A Thousand Words

A SWEET CHRISTIAN ROMANCE

UNFAILING LOVE SERIES PREQUEL

MANDI BLAKE

A Thousand Words
Unfailing Love Series Prequel
By Mandi Blake

Copyright © 2021 Mandi Blake
All Rights Reserved

No part of this book may be used or reproduced in any manner whatsoever without written permission, except in the case of brief quotations embedded in critical articles and reviews. The unauthorized reproduction or distribution of this copyrighted work is illegal. No part of this book may be scanned, uploaded or distributed via the Internet or any other means, electronic or print, without the author's permission.

This book is a work of fiction. The names, characters, places, and incidents are products of the writer's imagination or have been used fictitiously and are not to be construed as real. Any resemblance to persons, living or dead, actual events, locale or organizations is entirely coincidental. The author does not have any control over and does not assume any responsibility for third-party websites or their content.

Published in the United States of America
Cover Designer: Amanda Walker PA & Design Services
Editor: Editing Done Write

Contents

1. Sissy — 1
2. Tyler — 11
3. Sissy — 20
4. Tyler — 26
5. Sissy — 35
6. Tyler — 46
7. Sissy — 63
8. Tyler — 72
9. Sissy — 89
10. Tyler — 95
11. Sissy — 111
12. Tyler — 128
13. Sissy — 139
14. Tyler — 149
15. Sissy — 158
16. Tyler — 172
17. Sissy — 181
18. Sissy — 189
19. Tyler — 197
    Epilogue — 208

Other Books By Mandi Blake — 213
About the Author — 217
Acknowledgments — 219
Just As I Am — 221

CHAPTER 1
Sissy

Sissy's heart beat wildly, as if someone was banging against the walls of her chest. Her deep breaths were coming faster, and she tried to remember to inhale through her nose and exhale through her mouth. Coach Painter used to chant that helpful tip during softball practice back in high school.

Feeling too young to be this winded so early on in the game, she pushed harder as she neared the finish line—a rust-stained privacy fence at the back of the Wilsons' yard. She'd have to consider purchasing a gym membership if a ten-year-old outran her.

"Go, go, go! You've got him beat!" Claire screamed from somewhere behind Sissy.

Ahead, Jared faced her with his arms reaching out to his sides—one for Sissy and one for Cody, who raced beside her. His quick steps set a pace for her to match if she wanted to beat the kid in the sprint across the yard.

With a wide smile that strained her cheeks, Sissy slapped Jared's hand and tried to slow her all-out run. Cody collided with the fence seconds before Sissy did the same. Her open palms stung against the wood where she tried to brace herself for the impact.

Hoots and cheers mingled in the yard. She couldn't figure out who'd won over all the yelling.

Jared lifted Cody's hand like a referee in a boxing ring. The commotion the kids made over the race could rival a prime time title fight.

"She had you!" Claire yelled with a finger pointed at her older brother, Cody.

A triumphant smile spread across the kid's face. "When? Because I'm pretty sure she ate my dust."

Sissy propped her hands on her hips. "Wait just a minute. I think eating your dust is a little much."

"Winner, winner, chicken dinner," Cody chanted as he did a celebratory dance. He had decent moves for a kid.

"Okay. I can be a good loser," Sissy said. "I'll just remember that I always beat you at Pictionary."

Cody playfully glared at her. "That game is rigged."

Sissy laughed and wrapped her arms around the kid before swinging him around in a circle.

Claire bounced on her toes as Sissy slowed the whirl to a stop. She and Cody staggered and held onto each other as they tried to regain their balance.

"My turn! My turn!" Claire cried. Her strawberry-blonde curls fluttered as she hopped.

Sissy stumbled over to Claire who giggled in delight as they spun around.

"Mom!" Jared shouted as he dashed across the yard.

Sissy slowed the twirl to a stop and set Claire's feet on the ground before looking for Dr. Wilson. She was home earlier than Sissy had expected.

"Hey!" Sissy raised her hand in greeting as the rest of her body fell to the ground like a log.

The kids laughed as Sissy shook the dizziness from her vision. Thankfully, the Wilsons had an over-landscaped yard with that fluffy grass that seemed to stay pretty year-round, so the fall hadn't caused any damage.

Claire giggled as she stumbled to her mother. "Mommy!"

Marie Wilson wrapped her daughter in a tight hug. "Hey, sweet pea."

Claire kissed her mother's cheek before running away. "I'm not done playing!"

Sissy stood and wiped a few stray blades of grass from her jean shorts. "I didn't expect you back until later."

Sissy watched the Wilson kids almost every weekday after school, until Marie and David got home from work. Every once in a while, she got a call to babysit on the weekends. Today, the Wilsons had gone to lunch with some friends.

Marie stood to her full height and greeted Sissy with a smile. "Denise got a call from their daughter during lunch. She was having contractions, and they decided to head on over to the hospital." Marie shrugged. "It's their first grandbaby, so they're excited."

Marie and David were in their early fifties with young kids who weren't near the age of giving them grandkids. Sissy still had a hard time picturing her boss's friends having grandkids already. The Wilsons' kids were siblings they adopted a few years ago after enduring decades of infertility struggles.

Sissy rested her hands on her hips, still trying to catch her breath from the race and the twirling. "I bet they're over the moon."

Marie tilted her head toward the house while keeping her attention on the kids. "Come on in. Let me get your payment for the week."

Sissy followed Marie inside. The Wilson's home was a Carolina-blue Victorian built in the early 1900s, and Sissy had fallen in love with it when Marie had hired her to redesign the kitchen and dining room two years ago.

Sissy had a favorite room in almost every house she worked on, and the kitchen won that title for the Wilson's house by a landslide. Her favorite colors were silvers and pale blues. When Marie and David had agreed to this design, Sissy knew she'd be saving it for her own house one day. Even if she felt lightyears away from getting her own house and settling down with a family, she could always dream.

Marie sniffed the air. "It smells amazing in here."

"We made cookies. Would you believe the boys helped?"

"No, I don't believe it. I'm also reluctant to try them now."

Sissy laughed and swiped the cookie crumbs from the kitchen table into her hand.

"How were the kids today?" Marie asked as she opened the sub-zero fridge.

"Perfect. Claire ate her entire peanut butter and jelly sandwich."

Marie handed Sissy a bottle of water. "Good. I know she'll eat when she's hungry, but sometimes I worry about her size." Claire had a small build, even for a six-year-old, and her appetite was sometimes non-existent.

Sissy sat on a barstool where she had a clear view of the kids in the backyard and chugged the water. Georgia summers were brutal, and she spent a quarter of the afternoons reapplying sunscreen on the kids. Her own dark complexion wasn't as prone to burning, but she slathered the sunscreen on herself a few times a day just in case.

"Any plans this weekend?" Marie asked as she pulled a wallet out of her purse.

"You're lookin' at 'em."

"No dates?" Marie's eyes squinted the slightest fraction, giving Sissy a pitying look.

Sissy waved a dismissive hand. "It's fine. I think I've had enough first dates to last me through the decade." She wasn't sure how she felt about the dating scene, but she *was* tired of the long string of bad dates she'd been on this year.

"Not every date is going to end up with your drink in his face," Marie assured.

Sissy chuckled and covered her cheeks with her hands. Her skin was too tan to show much of a blush, but the mention of her last disaster of a date had her face heating up.

"Don't get me wrong. He deserved it," Marie said as she handed Sissy a few bills.

Sissy accepted the payment and tucked it into her pocket. "I know. I still feel bad about the mess I made. Not all of it landed on his face." She'd hung around to help the waitress clean up while apologizing profusely. She left an extra-generous tip when she paid the full dinner bill, and the waitress had been nice enough to pack up her meal to go.

Marie tilted her chin up. "He deserved every drop, and I expect you to continue to stand your ground when a man proposes something like that on the first date."

Sissy rested her forehead on the cool counter, unwilling to look at Marie after she brought up the crude things that guy had talked about.

Lifting her head, Sissy made a clicking noise behind her teeth. "I'm starting to wonder if guys are just like that these days. Dating is so fast paced, and everyone is..." She couldn't even finish the sentence. Sissy was strong in her faith in the Lord and in her commitment to waiting until marriage for anything physical beyond a kiss, yet the guy had been blunt about what he expected to happen after dinner. He'd practically asked for the sweet tea she'd tossed his way.

"Don't settle," Marie said sternly. "What about Christy? Any plans with her?"

"I'm sure we'll do something. There's a new movie she's been talking about."

Sissy's roommate, Christy, was a huge movie buff, and they usually ended up at the theater at least once a month.

It wasn't that Sissy minded hanging out with her roommate. She just preferred romantic comedies. Christy watched anything and everything, and that usually included crude humor or violence that made Sissy's stomach turn.

A small wrinkle formed between Marie's brows as she studied Sissy. "You know, there's a man I work with that might be a good match for you."

Sissy straightened. "Really?" She loved the fun side of dating, just not the train wrecks. And she was a huge romantic. She hadn't grown out of the fairytale phase of her childhood, and she could binge watch the Hallmark channel, despite Christy's critiques of the made-for-TV movies.

"I don't know why I didn't think of it before. He's a gentleman, he's intelligent, and he's a Christian." Marie's eyes widened. "He's perfect for you."

"Sounds like my kinda man. You know, the ones who are too good to be true."

"Tyler is a sweetheart." Marie tapped on her phone

before looking up. "But he can be a bit gruff at times. He's not rude or anything. Just a little too serious sometimes."

"Oh." Sissy's excitement faded. She knew all about Type-A men. They tended to be more put out by her free spirit than romantically interested.

Marie placed a hand over Sissy's. "I wouldn't suggest it if I didn't think the two of you might truly work out. He needs someone like you to nudge him out of his comfort zone."

"That's the thing. I've been down that road before. It leads to a dead end." Sissy propped her elbow on the counter and watched the kids in the backyard with her chin in her hand.

"Oh, come on. If anyone can show him a good time, it's you."

"Yeah, but serious people don't always like me. I'm their worst nightmare."

Marie chuckled. "You're serious about the things that matter. You're great at taking care of the kids. I never worry about them when you're here. You pay your bills on time, you change the oil in your car, and you're a wonderful business woman." Marie held up her hands, indicating the stunning kitchen. "You did a better job on this house than most professionals could have done."

Once again, Sissy was thankful her friend Brian's mom had introduced her to Marie when she first moved to Atlanta for college.

"How about I tell him about you on Monday, and

the two of you can have some time to think about it or text before you consider meeting up?"

Sissy tilted her head back and forth as she considered. "Okay. You can give him my number if he's interested."

"I just sent his to you. Just so you'll know who's calling."

"Thanks for this. I am kind of excited. You said you work with him?"

Marie leaned on the island. "He's a doctor at the clinic. He's in his last year of residency."

Sissy's brows lifted. "Impressive. I'm not sure what I'll have in common with a doctor, though."

"You get along with me just fine," Marie reminded her.

"That's true. What does he look like?"

Marie grinned. "He's handsome. Probably about twenty-eight years old. Medium-brown hair and dark eyes."

"You had me at Christian and handsome," Sissy said, rising from the barstool. "I hope that means his clothes won't be tea stained by the end of dinner."

"Great." Marie placed a hand on Sissy's shoulder and gave it an affectionate squeeze. "I'm excited for you. I can't believe I didn't think of this before."

"Probably because I have a new terrible date story every time I see you."

Marie nodded. "And I can't see Tyler being anything but kind to a woman on a date. Yep, I think this is a great idea."

Sissy hugged Marie. "Thanks again."

"Anytime. I'm proud of you."

Sissy leaned back. "For what?"

"For not giving in. I admire you for sticking to your morals. You're special, and I'm glad you aren't giving up on finding that special someone that the Lord will send just for you."

Sissy shrugged. "You know what they say. Fall down seven times, stand up eight."

"That's my girl." Marie patted Sissy on the back. "See you Monday."

CHAPTER 2

Tyler

Tyler walked out of the exam room and handed the file to Bethany at the nurse's desk. She didn't look up. Thankfully, the nurses only spoke to him if they had a question. They'd gotten the hint during his second month at the clinic that he wasn't here to chitchat.

He walked around the corner, heading toward his office, when Lisa moved into his path.

His instinct was to not engage at any cost, so he stepped to the right to move past her.

She slid in front of him, more deliberately blocking his path, and propped her hands on her hips, ready to lay into him about something.

"Mrs. Corners just left. She was in tears," Lisa spat. "What did you do to her?"

Tyler held his ground. "Nothing." At least, not anything he could recall, but others often disagreed with him about the way he said things. As if there was a difference in saying "You have congestive heart failure, and you're going to die if you don't exercise" in a sweet voice or in his usual, direct manner. The words still had the same meaning.

Lisa's scowl deepened. "I'm tired of your attitude." She pointed a bony finger at his face. "Stop hurting my friends' feelings."

"Not every patient is your friend," Tyler said.

If looks could kill, Tyler would be a dead man. Lisa's laser-beam glare could cut him in half like a lightsaber.

"I've been working at this same desk for thirty years. I'm not gonna sit around and watch you run people off."

Dr. Wilson approached, and her stern expression had Tyler straightening his shoulders. He respected her, and the last thing he wanted was to get on her bad side.

"Can the two of you take this somewhere else?" she asked in a tone that sounded as if she were telling instead of asking. "People in the parking lot can hear you two bickering."

Lisa glared at Tyler. "I think we're done here."

"I'm sorry, Dr. Wilson. It won't happen again," Tyler added.

Lisa gave a loud, sarcastic chuckle as she stepped back into the front office.

Tyler continued to his office, hoping the confrontation was over.

Dr. Wilson followed him, closing the door behind her. "We need to talk."

Did anything good ever follow that phrase? It typically marked the end of a relationship, and he didn't want to diminish his professional connection with Dr. Wilson.

"Please have a seat." Tyler indicated the extra chair in his office. Dr. Wilson had sat there a few times, but those conversations had been academic. He had a feeling this one was business related. "How can I help you?"

Dr. Wilson straightened her posture and crossed her legs at the ankles. She was a vision of professional excellence. "You have to work on your bedside manner."

Her words were exactly what he'd expected, but he rubbed his chin in thought. He wasn't the friendliest, but what did that matter, as long as he did his job well? Why was it considered a bad thing that he didn't beat around the bush?

"I appreciate you pointing it out to me. I'm aware that my rapport with the patients isn't the best." He looked her in the eye, hoping she would see his sincerity. "I'll work on it."

"Your compliance is appreciated. People come here when they're not feeling their best, and ideally, they should leave feeling assured in the treatment they've received."

"I understand." He could agree with her statement. He'd make a point to be friendlier to the next patient he saw.

She linked her hands together and rested them on his desk. "Now, I want to talk to you about a date."

"I beg your pardon?" He wasn't aware of any important dates coming up. Had he overlooked a charity event he'd promised to attend?

"I have a friend who I think you would like. She's funny, kind, and she's a Christian."

Tyler held up a hand. "You mean a date, as in dinner?"

"Dates sometimes include conversation over dinner, yes."

Tyler shook his head. "I don't mean to be rude, but—"

"Then don't. Take my advice and ask the girl out—to dinner, if that's what you prefer—but I'd like to remind you that there are other date options."

"I don't date," Tyler said resolutely. Medical school didn't leave much time for extracurricular activities, and he gladly accepted that role. Making friends and dating had never been one of his strengths.

Dr. Wilson cleared her throat. "Let me give you some advice. If you don't learn to have a better work-life balance, you'll never improve your bedside manner."

"I don't see what dating has to do with my job," Tyler said.

"More than you understand, apparently. I've

known this woman for a while, and she has everything you're missing in social skills."

"I don't need social skills to diagnose and treat patients."

Marie chuckled. "Yes, you do. You're so closed off, you have no idea what's actually going on in their lives. I'm often led to the answers to my patients' problems by something they revealed to me in casual conversation."

"I don't have time for that," Tyler said.

"I suggest you make time for it, Dr. Hart." She stood and reached for a sticky note and pen on his desk before writing a number on it. "This would be a great time to take the advice of someone who is older and wiser than you. Call her. She has a lot to offer."

Tyler accepted the note but didn't look at it. "Thank you, Dr. Wilson. I'll keep that in mind."

"It was a pleasure speaking with you as always," she said as she excused herself from his office.

He scanned the number written in Dr. Wilson's slanted handwriting. She hadn't even left a name.

Was this a matchmaking or an intervention? It didn't matter. He was opposed to either. He stuck the paper to the keyboard tray of his desk and began dictating notes from his last exam.

Three minutes later, he was in another exam room with an elderly man. A blood test revealed Tyler's suspicions were correct. The man had shingles.

Explaining the diagnosis and treatment should be

simple. Tyler wrote the man a prescription and sent him on his way with a handshake.

Bethany didn't speak to Tyler as he dropped off the chart, and Lisa didn't harass him in the hallway.

He didn't need a date to do his job well. The healing arts were a science, not an art.

By the end of the workday, the phone number Dr. Wilson had given him had made its way to the bottom of a stack of dozens of other, more important notes.

* * *

Tyler had just finished reading an article from the *Journal of American Medical Association* when his cell rang. His mother called every Thursday morning like clockwork.

Saving the article to reference later, he answered, "Hello."

"Hey. How's your week been?"

The purpose of his mother's call was always to ask him when he was coming to visit. While his parents only lived an hour from his place in Atlanta, the drive to and from Carson every weekend seemed like a waste of two hours he could be studying.

"Fine. And yours?" Tyler looked out the window to see the sun rising over the city. He opened the bottom right drawer of his desk and pulled out a protein bar for breakfast.

"Good. Your dad is building a gazebo in the backyard, so he's been busy."

"Does he need help?" Tyler asked.

Although he had a number of friends who still lived in Carson who would lend his dad a hand on a moment's notice, Tyler knew his parents would prefer his help under the guise of getting him home for the weekend.

"Oh no. Dakota comes by in the evenings," his mother said. "They're just working on it a little at a time, but I think they're almost finished."

His parents were retired, and it wasn't a secret that they were growing restless as empty nesters. His mom started volunteering at the botanical gardens, and his dad had taken up archery. Two things they hadn't shown any interest in while Tyler and his brother, Ian, had been living at home.

"Are you sure he doesn't need my help?" Tyler offered. It wasn't as if he had any plans this weekend—or any other, for that matter.

"I'd rather you wait until it's finished. We're hoping to have some friends over for a backyard get-together."

His mom had also perfected her hostess skills in the last few years. She was becoming a regular Carson socialite, as if being a *somebody* in a small town meant anything.

"Sure. Just let me know when."

Someone knocked on his office door, and Tyler looked up from his laptop to see Dr. Wilson standing in the open doorway with a scowling Lisa as her sidekick.

"Can I call you back?" Tyler asked his mother.

"Sure. I'll be around. Bye."

Tyler disconnected the call and checked the time. The clinic wouldn't open for half an hour.

He stood to greet the doctor and the office manager. "Good morning, Dr. Wilson. Lisa." He nodded once for each of them.

Though Lisa appeared to be biting her tongue, Dr. Wilson spoke first.

"We've had four patient complaints this week."

Tyler admired Dr. Wilson's directness. It was best to let her finish her piece before he responded. There was a chance the reason for their visit didn't have anything to do with Lisa's personal complaints with him.

Dr. Wilson crossed her arms over her chest. "Or should I say *you've* had four patient complaints this week. It's Thursday. They were all almost identical. Your demeanor with the patients must improve. Quickly."

Tyler nodded, conceding to the senior doctor's demand. "Yes, doctor."

Lisa's scowl morphed into a triumphant smirk, and she lifted her chin and walked away.

Dr. Wilson remained in the office doorway, waiting. "You still have the number I gave you?"

"I'll call her," Tyler said.

Unease boiled in his middle as Dr. Wilson excused herself without a farewell. He didn't believe the problem with his bedside manner was actually a problem. His approach was just different, but Dr. Wilson and Lisa seemed to be unwilling to let it go.

Tyler returned to his desk and shuffled the notes around in his keyboard drawer until he found the one he was looking for. Dr. Wilson was acting as if this contact was his lifeline, but she hadn't even left a name.

He wouldn't call her. He'd text her. Texting was informal, and he didn't want this alleged miracle worker getting the wrong idea. He had little time for social experiments and even less for pointless dates.

CHAPTER 3
Sissy

At ten minutes after eight on Saturday morning, Sissy stuck two slices of bread into the toaster and called Marie. Switching the call to speaker, Sissy laid the phone on the counter while she pulled raspberry jelly and strawberry preserves from the fridge.

"Hello," Marie answered, sounding tired.

"Good morning, doctor. Guess what?"

Marie hummed for a moment before saying, "Don't make me guess."

"He texted me!" Sissy squealed. "We're going to dinner tonight."

"Oh. Dinner." Marie sounded less than thrilled. "That's nice."

Sissy opened the jars and pinched the ends of the freshly toasted bread to sling it onto the plate. She sucked her burning fingertips.

"Mm-hmm. He's taking me to *Fireside*." Sissy

enunciated the name of the restaurant. A fancy place with white tablecloths seemed to deserve a drawn-out introduction.

"Wow. That *is* nice. Is he picking you up?"

Sissy looked around the tiny kitchen she shared with Christy. Their place wasn't anything to write home about, but they were in college and tried to save money whenever they could. Besides, who needed more than this?

"Actually, I'm meeting him at the restaurant."

Marie huffed. "He should've offered to pick you up."

"He did. He truly did," Sissy clarified. "I'm the one who suggested we meet at the restaurant."

"You wanted an escape vehicle?" Marie asked.

"Something like that. I like surprises, so I wanted it to be a blind date."

Marie laughed, and Sissy heard Claire giggle on the other end of the call.

"You're a card, you know that?" Marie asked.

"As long as you mean a wild card and not the Old Maid."

"Of course, dear. I think this will be a good surprise for both of you."

Sissy licked jelly off her fingers and tossed the knife into the sink. "I also asked him not to send me a photo."

"A *real* blind date," Marie specified. "I can't believe Tyler agreed to that."

"Mm-hmm. I didn't send him any pictures either.

It might do him some good to wonder about what I look like. He'll expect the worst, and I'll show up looking fabulous."

"Well, I already told him you were cute."

Sissy leaned on the counter and watched a bird peck at the birdfeeder in her backyard. "Yeah, but cute is a relative term."

"He'd be crazy not to like you," Marie assured.

"I also told him my name was Melanie so he can't search me on social media." She stuffed a bite of the raspberry toast into her mouth.

"That's a great idea. I can tell you've had your fair share of bad dates."

"Yep, and I didn't learn the name trick until one too many weirdos found me on social media."

Technically, Melanie was her real name, but everyone knew her as Sissy. Marie only knew Sissy's real name because she wrote it on her paycheck.

A crash sounded on Marie's end of the call, and she sucked in a breath through her teeth.

"Do you need to go handle that?" Sissy asked.

"No, I don't think there's any blood. So back to the date. How are you going to recognize each other at the restaurant?"

"Well, I asked him to wear a red rose boutonniere."

"You did not," Marie said in a low, disbelieving tone. "And he still agreed to the date?"

"He did. You must have really talked me up." She took another bite of toast. This time, she chose the strawberry. Variety was the spice of life.

"I told him he could learn a thing or two from you."

"I'm not sure what you mean by that, but I'm going to take it as a compliment."

Marie laughed, and Claire mimicked her mother with a giggle. "It's a compliment. If he can't have fun with you, he's doomed. I hope you have a great time."

"Yeah, about that. I was actually calling to see if you could maybe point me in the direction of something appropriate to wear to this swanky, highfalutin eatery."

"Claire and I will be over in about an hour and a half. I'll leave the boys with David."

"Do you know you're my favorite?" Sissy professed.

"I do. See you in a few."

Christy stepped into the kitchen just as Sissy ended the call.

She cheerfully greeted her roommate. "Good morning, sunshine!"

Christy squinted her eyes and grunted, "Too early."

Sissy pointed to an empty mug sitting beside the fresh coffee. "I made you something special."

"I love you," Christy muttered as she grabbed the carafe and poured a cup. She closed her eyes, inhaling the steaming drink.

"Love you too, friend. Toast?" Sissy offered.

"Nah, I'll grab a biscuit on my way to class. Are we on for a movie tonight?"

Sissy straightened. "You're looking at a woman who has a real, fancy date tonight...with a *doctor*."

"Shut the front door! How'd you manage that?"

"Marie hooked me up, but I intend to do some hooking myself if he plays his cards right." Sissy frowned. "Wait. That came out sounding different than I meant."

Christy lazily chuckled. "Relax. I know you're not hooking up or 'hooking' on the street. You're the last person I'd expect to pull a *Pretty Woman*."

"Thanks. I think," Sissy paused, unsure if her friend meant she wouldn't be mistaken as a prostitute or that she was a poor girl who couldn't catch the unwavering affection of a wealthy workaholic.

"Have fun, and remember the safe word," Christy reminded her.

They'd come up with a safe word after they'd both experienced their first terrible dates. If either of them texted the word pineapple, the other was to call with an emergency and provide an excuse to ditch the date.

It was another reason Sissy insisted on driving herself to dates. Once, she'd been forced to endure an entire date where the guy went on and on about how he couldn't wait to have a daughter one day. When she'd jokingly asked what he'd do if he ended up with a son instead, he'd given her a funny look and assured her that he wouldn't.

Then she'd listened to his ramblings on the ride home. It was weird, and she would do anything to avoid a similar situation in the future.

Sissy opened the fridge and grabbed a bottle of water for herself before tossing one to Christy. "Thanks. I hope I won't have to use it."

Christy caught the bottle with her free hand. "Same. Catch ya later."

Sissy scarfed down the rest of her toast and ran to her room to clean up. She had a few errands to run and an entire house to clean before Marie and Claire showed up.

CHAPTER 4

Tyler

Tyler rubbed a finger under his stiff collar. Sweat was already sliding down his back, despite the air conditioner in his car blowing gale-force winds. Atlanta summers could be unforgiving.

He pulled up to the valet parking desk and adjusted the flower on his lapel. Why had she insisted on this ridiculous marker? It meant he had to wear his suit jacket inside.

Stepping out of his inconspicuous gray pickup truck, he handed the keys to the valet attendant. He tucked the return card in the inner pocket of his jacket and pulled out his phone. A text from Melanie lit up the screen.

Melanie: I'm here. I'm wearing a dress to match your rose.

Tyler tilted his head down to eye the crimson flower on his chest. She was probably a woman who liked to flaunt her looks, and that wasn't going to go over well with him tonight.

The smell of roasted meat and spices filled his senses as he stepped into Fireside. He'd never been here before, but his friend Brian's dad had recommended the place and promised the steak was the best in the Southeast.

Tyler glanced past the hostess desk at the formal dining room. White tablecloths, low lighting, and mahogany accents set a soft, romantic vibe. He should have been clearer about his intentions for the evening when he asked for dinner date suggestions.

A dark-haired hostess straightened her shoulders and smiled when he entered. "Good evening. How many will be dining with you today?"

Tyler looked past her into the restaurant. "I'm meeting someone here. She's already seated."

His gaze landed on a red dress—the only one in the restaurant—and his eyes grew wide.

"Sir, do you see your dinner companion?" the hostess asked.

It was impossible. There was no way he'd set up a *date* with Sissy Calhoun. The Sissy Calhoun he'd grown up with and known his entire life.

But he was meeting Melanie here. That couldn't be right.

The hostess tilted her head, giving him a concerned look. "Sir, are you okay?"

He wasn't sure. He turned back to Sissy, and everything clicked into place. Her real name was Melanie.

He knew that, but everyone had always called her Sissy. They called her that because Tyler's friend, Dakota, was her brother. He'd called her Sissy since she was born, and so had all of their friends.

He couldn't take his eyes off her as the wheels spun in his head. Her dark hair hung in waves over one shoulder, and the color of her modest gown matched the rose on his chest perfectly. The silky, flowing material gathered around her ankles that were crossed and tucked beneath her chair.

Her innocent laugh carried through the restaurant, overpowering the soft music. A smiling waitress stood beside the table. Sissy cradled the woman's hand in hers, obviously admiring her manicure.

Of course Sissy had already made friends with the waitress.

"Sir?" the hostess asked again.

When the waitress left to check on another table, Sissy lifted a glass of water to her lips, and he watched the rolling movements of her neck as she swallowed.

Tyler turned to the hostess. "I'm sorry. I've just had something come up. Would you please tell my date that there was an emergency, and I won't be able to meet her tonight?"

He risked a glance at Sissy—his date that should never have been—and hastily pulled a large bill from his wallet. The hostess might catch an earful for being his scapegoat tonight, and she deserved compensation.

"Here. She's the woman in the red dress." He tilted his head toward the dining room.

"Sir..." the hostess began.

She wasn't taking the bill from his hand, and he didn't have time for this. His gaze darted back to Sissy in time to see her slowly look over her shoulder.

It was too late. Her gaze caught his, and a knowing smile spread across her face. It was like a firework against a dark summer sky.

Tyler's throat was dry. His fight-or-flight instincts were jammed, leaving him paralyzed.

Sissy stood, delight sparkling in her expression that had no business being there. She laid her hand on the silver clutch that rested on the table and took a step toward him.

Tyler shoved the bill at the hostess who was engrossed in the cat-and-mouse game that had just begun. As soon as her fingers wrapped around the bill, he sprinted to the door.

The humid air hit his face, and he caught sight of the valet attendant, but the man who had driven off with his getaway vehicle minutes ago was nowhere in sight.

He approached the valet podium just as a familiar voice pierced through the city noise.

"Tyler Hart!"

He wanted to crawl into a hole and disappear. Were there any manholes nearby?

The voice behind him was closer this time. "Tyler *Hart*," Sissy said, emphasizing his last name as if she were putting two and two together.

"Sissy," Tyler murmured as he rubbed his forehead. This was a nightmare, and he wanted out.

She stepped up beside him and propped her elbow on the valet podium. She was almost a foot shorter than his six-foot-two. "Fancy meeting you here. I'm meeting a hot doctor for a date tonight. Have you seen him?"

He didn't care if the hole was full of lizards and toads, he really wanted a place to hide right now.

She slid her fingers beneath the rose on his lapel and leaned in to smell it. Tyler sucked in a breath and regretted it instantly. Her hair smelled like a Tahitian beach.

She rose up and lifted her chin. He made the mistake of making eye contact, and every muscle in his body tensed.

"Long time no see, Dr. Hart. Going somewhere?" she asked. Her tone was low enough that he picked up the swirling of her emotions.

Sissy was never soft-spoken. Her volume dial was stuck on eleven, and the hushed tone of her voice sent a wave of gooseflesh over his arms. He felt it from his spine down to his toes.

What was happening to him? He'd never felt so trapped in his life, but his instinct to flee from the intimidating sprite beside him was being overtaken by intrigue. He hadn't expected his friend's little sister to evoke such a physical response.

Dakota's sister. She was Dakota's sister—the friend he'd talked to just this morning.

"Well," Sissy continued. "It seems I owe Dr. Wilson a thank you. She has great taste."

Tyler's cheeks heated. This was why he didn't date. It always ended badly.

He cleared his throat. His mouth was dry, and the sweat beneath his collar was getting worse. "Listen, we should just forget this ever happened. I'm sorry for the inconvenience."

Sissy linked her arm with his, hooking them together. "Oh, no. I ordered an appetizer, and I'm not leaving until I get a steak. Plus, I got all dressed up." She slid a hand down the side of her red dress.

Tyler resisted. "This is absurd. Why didn't you use the name you go by?"

Sissy huffed. "Because there are creepers out there. A lady knows better than to tell a random stranger too much about herself. Also, it *is* my name."

Okay, he couldn't fault her for that. The thought of Sissy ending up on a date with a psycho had his jaw tensing. He wouldn't approve of her dating someone who committed tax fraud either. It was actually a long list that he didn't want to think about right now.

Sissy tugged on his arm, and he resisted again. "We really shouldn't." He somehow couldn't verbalize informative sentences when Sissy was touching him.

"Why not?" she asked.

He wished he had half of her confidence. She looked him dead in the eye with determination, and he found his reasoning growing weak.

"Because," he finally supplied.

Great. Now his intelligence had completely abandoned him. Almost a decade of higher education was useless in front of Sissy Calhoun.

Sissy shook her head. "I don't think so. Can't you cooperate for one evening of fun?"

She tugged on his arm, and he didn't resist this time.

"We shouldn't," he said, looking around for someone to save him from the tempting woman leading him back inside the restaurant.

He was not allowed to think of her as a woman. She was his friend's sister, way too young for him, and they had nothing in common. He had a million reasons to say no, and only one reason to say yes. Because Sissy told him to.

But for some reason, he wanted to let her lead him inside right now. He was terrified, and the adrenaline pumping through his veins was making his heart pound and his back sweat.

Sissy abandoned her leading and looked up at him with dark eyes he'd never noticed before now. "If you don't have fun with me tonight, you don't ever have to call me again."

Tyler slowly shook his head, but his brain wasn't telling his mouth what to say. He didn't like the idea of treating her to a date and never calling after. Sissy didn't deserve to be ghosted, even if she wasn't his type.

Dates were for getting to know each other, but he already knew a lot about Sissy. She'd never taken anything seriously in her life, much like most people her age. She was closer to twenty than his twenty-eight.

"Come on. Buy me a steak. I promise I won't choose the most expensive one," she joked.

Tyler was standing on the edge of a cliff, and his balance was wavering. Sissy had done an amazing job of taking him out of his element and sticking him in uncharted territory.

He was beginning to see why Dr. Wilson thought he had something to learn from Sissy. She forced him to adapt, but she also kept him on his toes. Sissy didn't have a filter, much less the capacity to analyze situations before diving in.

Dr. Wilson had described Sissy as cute, which was way off base. She was beautiful in the way polar bears were beautiful—nice to look at, dangerous to touch.

But she was friendly, as Dr. Wilson had promised. Sissy never met a stranger, and everyone loved her.

Except Tyler. He couldn't. Getting mixed up with Sissy Calhoun was more trouble than it was worth.

"Please," Sissy begged. "I won't order dessert."

Tyler huffed. "It's not about the money."

"Then come on. Our appetizer is probably waiting." She tugged his arm again.

"Sissy—" He stopped, unable to form an excuse. Thinking fast was a part of his job description, but she'd disabled his defenses.

She turned around, and his attention was drawn to the soft curve of her lips as they tugged into a knowing grin.

"We'll take it one word at a time," she said.

When had she found this voice that was comforting and assuring when he was completely out of his element?

None of this made sense. But as he looked from Sissy to the restaurant and back to her, his curiosity stirred to know the Sissy standing in front of him in the red dress.

Because this woman wasn't someone he knew, and that's why he took her hand and led her back inside.

CHAPTER 5

Sissy

Sissy bit the inside of her lip, trying to hide her grin. She was excited to find out she actually knew her surprise date, but Tyler was about to bust a blood vessel in his neck.

Tyler Hart was her hot doctor date. She did a little happy dance—in her mind, of course—because the dress she'd borrowed from Christy wouldn't allow any sudden movements.

She'd had her eye on the oldest Hart brother for the last ten years, but he'd never paid her any mind. Today, she had his full attention, and she wanted to spend every minute wisely.

Sissy kept her composure as Tyler's hand rested carefully on the small of her back. He led her straight past the hostess whose curious gaze followed them through the entrance. They'd managed to draw the attention of every patron in the restaurant. It wasn't every day she got to swing her hips into a fancy-schmancy restaurant next to a smoldering doctor.

Because that's what Tyler did. He smoldered. It was really his serious, stick-in-the-mud attitude, but he made it look good.

Neither of them spoke as he pulled her chair out. She slowly lowered into the seat, careful not to pull the dress in the wrong places. The whole evening was a test in grace. One wrong move would have her showing more than just her spirited attitude.

"Thank you." Sissy carefully laid the napkin across her lap. "So, how's the fam?"

"Good." Tyler scanned the dining room, no doubt searching for a waiter to interrupt the awkwardness.

"What are you thinking about?"

Tyler swallowed hard and took a sip from the glass of water sitting in front of him. "Dakota."

Sissy narrowed her eyes. "Eww. Stop it."

Tyler shrugged and took another gulp of water.

"Why are you thinking about my brother?" She'd selfishly hoped he was thinking about her, preferably how good she looked and how entertaining she was, despite the shock of finding out he'd known his blind date since elementary school.

He set the glass down and began drumming his knuckles against the table. The sound was muted by the thick tablecloth, but he might as well have been banging battle drums based on his overreaction to the date.

When he finally spoke, his gaze locked on her.

Tyler could be intimidating when he wanted to be, and his attention sent a thrill down her spine. "Because."

Dakota was her older brother, and he'd been the stern protector since their dad died. Tyler was a few years older than Dakota. Looking at the man sitting across from her, she knew Tyler was the kind of person her brother would *want* her to date. Kind, intelligent, and responsible. But she knew there was some kind of bro code that said a guy's best buds couldn't date his little sister.

So, she'd probably get some pushback from the overbearing brother, but he'd get over it. He had his own problems to take care of. Exhibit A: Sissy's best friend that he'd been hung up on since he was fourteen.

If he could break the no dating the sibling's friend rule, so could she. Sissy just intended to do a better job than Dakota. Lindsey had been gone a while now, and he still hadn't gotten over the woe-is-me stage of the breakup. Now Sissy was stuck walking on eggshells around two of the people who mattered the most to her.

"You're not afraid of my brother, are you?" There was a hint of challenge in her tone that was completely intended.

"No."

The waitress returned with a plate of bruschetta decorated with reds and greens that looked almost too pretty to eat.

"Wow. That looks delicious," Sissy said as she

wiggled her brows at Linda, the sweet woman she'd gotten to know while she waited for Tyler.

"I hope you enjoy it. Do you have any questions about the menu?" she asked with her hands carefully clasped behind her.

"I don't," Sissy said before looking at Tyler. "Are you ready to order?"

He nodded and lifted the menu.

"I'll have the eight-ounce ribeye, medium, with the parmesan crust and a side salad," Sissy said as she handed the waitress the menu.

"What kind of dressing would you like on your salad, Miss?"

Sissy made a thoughtful humming sound. "Surprise me."

"And for you, sir?"

Tyler didn't look up from the menu. "I'll have the filet, medium-well, with a loaded baked potato." He turned to Sissy as he handed the menu to the waitress. "Would you prefer a filet?"

Sissy shook her head. She could hardly tell the difference in cuts of meat, so a top-dollar steak would be wasted on her when she'd be just as satisfied with what she'd ordered.

Linda's genuine smile faltered when she dropped the menus onto the table, knocking Sissy's water glass over.

"I'm so sorry." Linda grabbed the fallen glass and pulled a cloth napkin from her apron.

Sissy stood and used her own napkin to wipe up some of the spill. "It's okay! No big deal."

Tyler held up his own napkin, and Sissy took it when hers and Linda's were thoroughly soaked.

"I'm sorry again," Linda said in a wavering voice.

Sissy rested her hand on Linda's shoulder. "It's really okay. It's just water. It didn't even get on anything except the table."

Holding the handful of wet napkins, Linda nodded. "I'll be right back with a new tablecloth and more napkins." She scurried off, still shaky from the spill.

Sissy rested back onto her seat. "That was exciting."

Tyler watched her with a look of interest now. It almost looked as if he were waiting for her to do something drastic. "Yes."

Sissy leaned over the table, pretending to share a secret with her date. She was a little miffed that he could string together three plus words for the waitress but not for her. "Have it your way. You can use your one-word answers, but I get to ask the questions."

Tyler leaned back in his chair and gave her a single nod to proceed.

Sissy settled in for the grilling. She had him right where she wanted him. "Boxers or briefs?"

Tyler's eyes widened, and his whole face turned the color of the rose clipped to his lapel. He'd actually worn the flower, which blew her mind.

She held up a hand. "Breathe, cowboy. I was joking. We'll talk about underwear later."

Tyler sat forward so fast his water sloshed up the sides of the glass. "Sissy."

"Stop it," she said with a wave of her hand. "I really am joking. You're so easy." She had no idea what kind of underwear any man wore, and she intended to keep it that way.

"Please," Tyler gritted, his expression pleading as earnestly as the single word.

"All right. I can keep it PG," Sissy promised. She held up two fingers, side-by-side. "Scout's honor."

"Three," Tyler corrected.

Sissy looked at her fingers and added another. "Whatever. I was never a Scout. You like sports?"

"Fishing."

She wanted to steer clear of that subject. Tyler and Dakota had been fishing buddies since middle school.

Sissy tapped her cheek in thought. "What's your favorite dessert?"

"Cheesecake."

She rolled her eyes. "That's about as plain as vanilla ice cream. Any toppings?"

"No."

"Spring or summer?"

Tyler raised one eyebrow.

"You don't get to give me that silent, judgmental look," Sissy said as she waved her finger. "I'm asking all the questions here."

"Spring."

He straightened his posture and crossed his arms over his chest. If he thought he could shut her out with a closed-off stance and one-word answers, he couldn't be more wrong.

"Are you a morning person or a night person?"

"Morning."

Sissy rested her elbows on the table. "Now we're gettin' somewhere."

Two waiters showed up and removed the wet tablecloth, replacing it with another.

When they were alone again, Tyler rubbed his forehead. "Sissy, do we have to do this? I still don't think it's a good idea."

She raised a hand to stop him. "We don't have to, but I'd love it if you humored me. If I didn't know better, I'd think you're in pain or something. I'm not asking you to sing karaoke or cut off your right hand."

Tyler averted his gaze and scanned the room. "Okay."

She was toeing a line here. If she wasn't careful, she'd scare him off.

Throughout the remainder of dinner, she kept the questions light and commented on the delicious food. She'd be leaving a raving review on Yelp when she got home tonight.

Linda returned later, and Sissy had flashed her most understanding smile enough that the waitress began to relax.

After their plates were removed, Tyler propped his arms on the table and asked, "Would you like dessert?"

Her eyes and smile grew wide. "You can speak in sentences!"

Tyler tilted his head as if he were irritated with her excitement.

"No, I will not have dessert," she said formally. In truth, she was proud of herself for expressing such self-control. Dessert was her favorite part of every meal, but she'd seen the lack of prices on the menu, and a slice of chocolate cake might cost more than her monthly rent payment.

He caught Linda's attention with a subtle tilt of his head. "Could we see the dessert menu?"

The ever-ready Linda pulled a small menu from her apron. "Our special tonight is bananas foster."

Tyler handed the menu to Sissy, silently giving her the go-ahead to choose.

She chewed her bottom lip as she scanned the menu. "I'd like the New York cheesecake, please."

The reaction was miniscule, but Sissy caught a small twitch in his brows as he handed the menu back to Linda.

When they were alone again, Tyler turned his full attention to her, and she found it hard to hold his gaze. He might stick to the sidelines, but it sent a thrill of excitement through her every time he scrutinized her.

"Why did you order cheesecake?" he asked.

Sissy shrugged. "I like cheesecake too."

"Yeah, but you'd probably have preferred the chocolate cake."

"Chocolate cake would be nice, but I wanted you to share it with me."

She watched as Tyler's chest rose and fell in huge waves with his deep breaths. Satisfied with her answer, he settled back in his chair. "How do you know Dr. Wilson?"

She tried not to read too much into the reversal of the question game, but she silently rejoiced. "Brian's parents introduced us when I moved here for college a few years ago. I helped with the interior design work when they bought their house, and I've been babysitting for them ever since."

Tyler's gaze was now glued to her. "Why did she set us up?"

"Because I'm fabulous, and you're quite a catch yourself."

The redness was spreading through Tyler's face again. It was adorable that his blush wasn't contained to his cheeks. It covered every inch of his face.

She did her best to steer the conversation into comfortable territory. The date was almost over, and they were entering the homestretch. If she played her cards right, she might actually win him over.

When dessert arrived, Tyler surprised her by picking up the second spoon and taking a small spoonful after each of her own bites. The evening was definitely getting a tally in the win column. She'd be calling her best friend, Lindsey, as soon as she got home.

Linda brought their check, and Tyler dismissed

Sissy when she offered to split the bill. She hadn't expected any less from Tyler, but she'd felt compelled to offer since he'd begrudgingly agreed to dinner with her.

When they stepped out onto the sidewalk, Tyler asked, "Where did you park?"

Sissy pointed to a lot about a block away, and Tyler tilted his head, urging her to lead the way. She'd made a point to move her clutch to the other side, leaving her hand dangling and free for him to take. He walked beside her but made no move to grab her hand. Too bad the hot doctor was too rigid to take the hint.

When they approached her car, Tyler cleared his throat beside her.

"What is it, Dr. Hart? Do you know which car is mine?" she asked.

Tyler gave her a narrow-eyed look that had her stomach flipping in delight.

When they reached her bold purple coupe, she unlocked the door before turning to him. "I had fun tonight."

His hands were in his pockets giving her no chance of a good-bye hug or anything interesting. Not that she'd kiss on the first date, but she was itching for some kind of reaction from him.

She continued, "No pressure, but please call me."

He didn't confirm or deny, but his jaw tensed. She hadn't decided if that was a promise or a dismissal. Since he didn't say no, she chose to believe it was closer to a yes.

She looked up at him and flashed her most comforting smile. "Can I have one more word tonight?"

Tyler reached around her to open the door of her car. "Good night."

She got two words, but they left her feeling defeated as she lifted the skirt of her dress and slid into the car.

CHAPTER 6
Tyler

Tyler finished dictating the report on his final patient of the day and glanced at his phone. He'd been waffling over Sissy's last request all day.

He could call her, but he shouldn't. He could text her, but he shouldn't. He would reach for the phone then shove it in his pocket when he changed his mind.

Certainty was his best friend. He dealt with enough gray areas in his line of work, and he didn't appreciate indecision in his personal life. Up until now, there hadn't been any. He knew his lane, and he stayed in it. Then Sissy came along, and he was swerving all over the road.

Nothing had to change. He should forget about his friend's little sister in that red dress—if only he could actually put that plan into practice. Images of Sissy from their dinner that was not a date played on repeat in his mind. The way she leaned forward when she challenged him, the waves of her dark hair that hung over her shoulder, and the various smiles she'd used as weapons throughout the evening. He'd counted six different smiles, and they each had a different meaning.

Why did she have to be so interesting? She had an alluring nature, always resilient and upbeat. He didn't notice her falter once until the absence of any smile at all when he'd told her good night.

If she'd thought she was getting a kiss, she could think again. There was no way he was kissing Sissy Calhoun.

It wasn't that he didn't want to because, surprisingly, he did. He just couldn't let things get twisted between them. He hadn't had a problem keeping things simple before. He hadn't seen Sissy in years, but it seemed everything had changed, including his reaction to her presence. He'd never been one to stumble over his words, until she shook him up at dinner.

Tyler rubbed his forehead, trying to wipe away the pestering thoughts of Sissy. A knock sounded at his office door, and he shoved his phone into the top drawer of his desk. If he couldn't see it, he wouldn't be tempted to call her.

"Come in."

Dr. Wilson stepped into his office. "Are you getting ready to leave for the day?"

"Yes, but I can hang around if you need something." It wasn't as if he had any plans tonight—or ever.

"Oh no. I just wanted to ask how your date went. I saw Sissy this morning when she showed up to babysit, but I was in a bit of a hurry and didn't get to catch up with her."

Tyler gestured for Dr. Wilson to have a seat before leaning his arms on the desk. He'd give her the Cliffs Notes version of the evening. "We actually know each other. We didn't realize it until we met at the restaurant."

"Oh, I had no idea." Dr. Wilson settled into a seat, intrigued and all ears for his story. "How do you know Sissy?"

"We grew up together."

"How sweet," Dr. Wilson crooned with a smile.

"Actually, it means the date was over before it began. Her brother is my friend, and I don't think he'd be too pleased to find out I went on a date with his sister."

Dr. Wilson's brows furrowed. "Why not?"

"Her brother is a good guy. He's very protective, and you failed to mention how young she was."

She waved a hand and scoffed. "That doesn't matter. She's a sweetheart."

"About that. She's... a little too much for me."

Dr. Wilson frowned. "That's exactly why I thought you would be good together. Sissy is friendly and genuine. She's unapologetically herself. I'm not sure you've ever stepped out of your comfort zone for anything. Did you at least treat her to dinner?"

"I did, but I wouldn't consider it a date."

"Why not? Did you not have a good time?"

Tyler rubbed his jaw for a moment as he thought. "I did, but nothing can come of it."

Dr. Wilson stood. "Well, I can see this talk isn't going anywhere. I'm sorry to hear things didn't work out."

Tyler turned his attention back to his computer. "I do appreciate the thought."

"Tyler."

He looked up to see Dr. Wilson standing in the doorway.

"I don't believe I was wrong. I still think Sissy would be good for you. I encourage you to reconsider."

Tyler nodded. "Thank you, doctor. I'll think about it."

He wouldn't. At least, his entire evening would be devoted to *not* reconsidering his stance on Sissy Calhoun. How successful he would be remained unknown.

"Have a nice evening." Dr. Wilson waved as she stepped out into the hallway.

The ride home from the office was loud. Between the warring thoughts in his head and the classic rock radio station he'd turned up, he didn't hear his phone dinging until he parked in front of his apartment.

When he picked up the phone, Sissy's name was listed twice in the notifications.

He opened the text and began reading.

Sissy: Hello, Doctor Hart.

Sissy: What are you doing?

Tyler rubbed his forehead and prayed aloud.

"Lord, please make her go away." Her name had been bouncing around in his head all day. He didn't need her messages showing up on his phone too.

He huffed and leaned his head back against the headrest. After banging it a few times, he picked up the phone and responded.

Tyler: Working.

He'd already left work, and he wasn't actually doing anything.

Her reply was almost immediate.

Sissy: What are you doing after work?

Tyler: Nothing.

Sissy: Good. Meet me here.

He read the address and considered leaving his phone in the car for the rest of the night. Instead, his traitorous fingers typed the message.

Tyler: Now?

Sissy: Yes. Chop Chop.

Tyler's heart began pounding. What was he doing? Seeing Sissy again would only make things worse. Why was he considering starting up the truck?

Tyler: Why?

Sissy: Stop texting me and start driving.

Tyler threw the phone into the passenger seat and hung his head in his hands. Why was she getting under his skin?

Sliding his fingers through his hair, he fisted his

hands and pulled. She literally made him want to pull his hair out.

He grabbed the phone anyway and clicked the address to move to the GPS. It was fifteen minutes away and in a part of town he'd never been to before. Actually, it wasn't in the Atlanta metropolitan area. It was just outside the city hub on his side of town. He rested the phone in the cupholder as the navigational voice directed him to proceed to the route.

The summer sky was brushed with bright oranges and deep purples as he pulled into the driveway of an old, two-story home. The white-painted wood on the house was chipping, and, while the front yard had recently been mowed, taller grass gathered around the bases of the Bradford pear trees that dotted the lawn.

Behind the house, a wide lake stretched to the far reaches of the other bank. Tyler scanned the road and the houses around it. How had he not known about this lake?

The only thing he recognized was Sissy's purple car. All was quiet as he climbed the steps onto the creaky porch. The bustle of the city didn't reach this place.

Sissy threw open the door before he had a chance to knock. "You came!"

Tyler questioned his judgment. Why *had* he come?

"Yeah," he said noncommittally.

She stepped toward him without warning, and before he knew it, he was backing up to put the space back between them.

The screen door closed behind her with a metallic slap. "You ready?"

No, he wasn't ready. He didn't even know what he was doing here besides obeying Sissy's beck-and-call.

"Where are we going?" he asked.

"Another sentence!" Sissy exclaimed as she walked down the stairs leading off the porch and around the left side of the house. "It's not far. I don't have long, but I thought you'd want to see this."

Tyler followed Sissy down the sloping path toward the lake. She wore a shimmery gold sleeveless shirt that reflected the waning sunlight with every move she made, but the brightness of her smile was radiant beyond the power of the sun. The vivid colors of the sky reflected in the calm water, and a large blanket was laid out on the wooden dock.

"Sissy," he said low and questioning as he followed her.

She turned to face him but continued walking backwards. "I was hanging out by the lake studying, and I thought of you."

"Me?" he asked.

"Yeah, I know you like fishing. Have you ever fished here?"

"No. I didn't even know it was here."

She stepped onto the blanket and sat beside a thick textbook. "Come on."

Tyler didn't make a move to sit as she leaned back, tilting her face to the warm sun.

"There's plenty of room to sit beside me without touching," she offered without opening her eyes.

She could make fun all she wanted, but he wasn't afraid of getting close enough to touch her. He was terrified of getting close enough to feel something.

Resigned to the plans Sissy had made for him this evening, he sat on the blanket beside her. He propped one knee up and rested his arm on it. The weather was perfect, and the smoothness of the lake was calming his racing heart.

He snuck a glance at Sissy. With her eyes closed, she looked so peaceful, and he could almost imagine this wrecking ball wasn't out to destroy any semblance of order he held in his life.

"Are you going to enjoy this, or are you going to sit there and mull over your excuses to leave?" she asked without moving.

It unnerved him when she perceived his mood. He sighed and looked out at the lake. "Do you live here?"

"No way. My roommate's parents live here. She works with them. She needed a ride home today, so I'm waiting around for her to get off work."

After a few seconds of silence, Sissy stood. She kicked off her sandals and sauntered along the edge of the dock. Her movements were fluid and graceful like the peaceful water around them.

She stepped to the end of the dock and peered into the water. Something held her attention as she studied it. When she screamed and pointed to the water below, Tyler sprang to his feet.

It was a snake. It had to be. Nothing else would elicit a reaction like that.

"Get back," he yelled, reaching for Sissy.

Sissy reached for him at the same time, but his dive toward her was overzealous. It all happened in the blink of an eye. Their combined body weight crashing into each other only served to quicken the fall. Her arms were tightly wound around him as they crashed into the water.

She released her hold on him as they hit. The whirling of bubbles and muted noises swirled around him as he searched for her. Where was she?

He spread his arms and fanned them out in an arc that propelled him to the surface. Once his head was above water, he turned left and right looking for her. "Sissy?"

A heartbeat later, she burst through the surface in front of him and wiped the water from her face, yelling, "Snake!"

Her dark hair looked impossibly black, but her ever-present smile was gone. They were in the enemy's territory now, and Tyler's instincts worked quickly. He grabbed Sissy's hand and pulled her to him. The water rushing between them lapped over his chest and neck as he wound his arm around her.

He scanned the gap between the water and the dock. "Where did you see it?"

Sissy pointed, and he narrowed his eyes to focus on the shape floating in the water.

Once he was sure of what he was looking at, he sighed. "Sissy, that's a stick."

"A stick!" she screeched.

He took a deep breath through his nose and exhaled through his mouth. "Yeah. Just a stick."

Sissy rested her forehead on his shoulder. "I'm sorry. That was stupid."

Tyler was still trying to calm his racing heart rate. The last thing he'd imagined for his evening was falling into a lake.

He definitely hadn't expected to get this close to Sissy. With his arm still around her, their bodies were flush against each other.

He brushed water from his face and sighed. "It's fine."

"You don't sound like it's fine," she whispered. "You sound upset."

"I just didn't plan on getting in the lake."

"Well, we're already here. Since we can't change it, why don't we enjoy it?" She pulled away and paddled her arms out to her sides to stay afloat, but a grin was spreading on her face.

"I'm in my work clothes, and my shoes are dragging me down."

"We can be wet and gripe about it, or we can be wet and enjoy it. Take your pick."

It was a simple thought that hadn't occurred to him. This was exactly what Dr. Wilson had been trying to get through to him. His tendency was to see the downside, but Sissy found the silver lining in everything. She was made of sunshine and rubber—bright and elastic enough to bounce back from anything.

"Give me a minute." He needed time to come to grips with Sissy's bubbly outlook on life.

He swam for the dock and held onto it with one hand. Reaching into the dark waters, he grabbed his waterlogged shoes one by one and threw them up.

He was still trying to catch his breath, but he needed something to hold onto—not to keep himself up, but an anchor.

Sissy floated nearby. The expression on her face was one of confusion as she studied him. He was irritated at the circumstances, not her.

Tyler sighed and reached for her arm. He pulled her closer and whispered, "You scared me." He'd been convinced she was standing too close to a snake that could be venomous. Cottonmouths and water moccasins were everywhere in the Central Georgia waters, and they weren't anything to mess around with if you wanted a fighting chance.

"There's no danger now," she said as she brushed her hair from her eyes.

He released her arm and his hold on the dock.

He looked her in the eye and stressed again, "You still scared me when you screamed. I thought you were in danger."

Sissy smiled and moved a little closer. "I wasn't, but thanks for coming to my rescue."

Every moment he spent with her required vigilance. Right now, she was lowering his walls with that small, sweet smile.

"Now," she said, moving even closer, "isn't this nice? The water is warm, and the sun is setting. It's so relaxing."

Nice was an understatement. Being this close to Sissy was exhilarating and tempting. "Sissy, we shouldn't—"

She touched his lips with her fingertip, and the gentle contact made them tingle.

"Shh. Don't talk about all the things we shouldn't do. Just enjoy this. The water feels amazing. Just breathe."

It was so intimate, so close, and it sparked an electrical force that shot through his body. He tried to obey, but his lungs were collapsing. He couldn't breathe when she was so close.

She brought her arms up and around his shoulders. An uncertain expression replaced her usual array of smiles. His arm naturally wrapped around her waist, holding them together.

"Hey," she whispered as if her unending stream of consciousness had been reduced to a single word.

Adrenaline surged through his body, tingling over his skin and racing through his veins. She was so close, so warm against him. They were nose to nose, and one small movement would seal her lips against his.

It was the last thing he wanted to admit, but she made him believe falling in a lake fully clothed wasn't so bad. In fact, he felt freer than he'd ever felt in his life.

Footsteps sounded on the dock, and they both

turned to see a woman approaching. Her arms were crossed over her chest, but her smile was wide. She was definitely entertained by catching Sissy and him in the water.

"Sorry to interrupt. Y'all look a little cozy."

Tyler released his hold on Sissy, breaking the trance.

"Perfect timing. You ready to go?" Sissy asked. "Oh, Tyler, this is my roommate, Christy. She already knows about you."

His face heated as he tried to school his voice to a formal tone. "It's a pleasure to meet you." Actually, it was a surprise to meet her. He didn't like making a first impression like this one. It was humiliating to have so little control.

"Good to meet you. Sissy says good things about you, *Doctor* Hart," she emphasized his title.

Sissy swam toward the bank. "Give me a few to get dried off and we can go."

Tyler followed her, realizing he was about to get his truck soaking wet.

Christy met them on the lakeshore and handed the blanket to Sissy. She rubbed it over her arms and legs before handing it to Tyler. While he did his best to dry off his arms, Sissy leaned to the side and squeezed water out of her thick hair.

There wasn't much to be done about his pants. They were soaked and dripping over his socked feet.

Christy handed the textbook to Sissy. "Do you have any extra clothes?" she asked.

He thought for a moment. "I do." He found it odd that he hadn't recalled the gym clothes in his truck until now. It took all the steam out of his irritation at falling in.

Sissy ran her fingers through her hair. "I don't, but it's fine."

Christy grabbed their shoes and nodded toward the house. "You can wear something of mine." She handed Tyler his shoes and wore a look that was almost sympathetic. "I'll show you where you can change."

The sky had turned mostly orange as they walked toward the house. Tyler grabbed his gym bag from the truck and pulled his wet socks off before following Christy into the house.

The inside looked just as he'd expected. Wallpaper and family photos covered the walls and hardwood floors ran through every room.

Christy stopped outside a room and gestured for him to enter.

"Thanks," he said as he stepped into the guest bath.

Christy stalled in the doorway. "Hey, you know Sissy likes you, right?"

Tyler's mouth quirked up on one side. He appreciated Christy's directness. He didn't like beating around the bush. "I know."

"I just... I guess I want you to give her a chance. She respects you, and from what she tells me, you're not like other guys."

Tyler's heart raced, but his brow furrowed. "How so?"

Christy's attention turned to the floor. "Sissy has a lot to offer, but most guys want more than she's willing to give."

Understanding clicked into place, followed by a wave of anger. "I would never take advantage of Sissy." Is that what Christy thought about catching them in the lake? They'd only been on one date. No, that wasn't a date, and tonight wasn't a date either.

He wouldn't even be kissing Sissy, much less anything else. Had someone else tried to take advantage of her? Anger flared and roared in his chest. Any man who pushed Sissy to do anything like that would have to answer to him and Dakota.

Dakota. Tyler had forgotten about her brother, and he added that important point back to the top of the list of reasons why he shouldn't have come here.

Christy smiled. "I didn't think you would. Just remember that she's special. Oh, and towels are in the closet." She closed the door, leaving him to change and dry off.

He tore off the wet clothes and dried off in a rush before throwing on the gym clothes he'd grabbed from the truck. Thankfully, he'd skipped the gym this morning, and the clothes were clean.

Sissy was waiting for him on the porch, and he could see Christy waiting in the passenger seat of Sissy's purple car.

Sissy had pulled her wet hair into a bun, and she

brushed a stray strand behind her ear. "Thanks for coming. I had fun. And I'm sorry again."

"It's fine." Tyler was shocked to realize his words were true. It was fine. He'd fallen into a lake, not a volcano. Sissy had taken the unfortunate fall and stripped the negativity from it. Christy's words were being played out for him in the light of the setting sun.

Just remember that she's special.

He wanted to reject the realization, but his mind knew otherwise. There was something special about Sissy, or maybe it was a dozen different things. She was a rainbow in a world of gray.

She *was* special. She *was* different. But those observations were muted when he remembered all of the reasons why they wouldn't work together.

Sissy playfully punched his shoulder. "See you next time, doc."

After holding hands and having her wrapped in his arms, a friendly shoulder shove was about twelve steps backwards. Maybe she understood and was trying to put a safe distance between them.

He climbed into the truck and watched Sissy's car back out and disappear down the road before he started the engine. He was halfway home before he realized he hadn't eaten since breakfast.

His phone started ringing when he pulled into the parking lot of a diner down the road from his house. Dakota's name lit up the screen.

Tyler silenced the ringer and rubbed his hand through his hair. It had mostly dried on the ride home, but the dampness reminded him that he'd been with Sissy less than half an hour ago.

He declined the call and typed up a message to his friend.

Tyler: Call you later.

Guilt tightened around his throat as he killed the engine and stepped out of the truck. He couldn't remember a time when he'd ignored a phone call from someone he knew. People often called him first if they needed help because he was sure to answer.

Today, he wasn't sure about anything, including how he felt about Sissy Calhoun.

CHAPTER 7

Sissy

Sissy tied the drawstring on her favorite sweatpants as her phone rang. Her hair was still wet from the shower, but she'd dry it after talking to Lindsey.

"I have good news," Sissy answered.

Lindsey sighed. "I need to hear those words. Tell me a story."

Sissy missed her best friend so much it hurt, especially on days like this when Lindsey sounded glum. She'd been in New York for a few years, and she was still struggling to catch a break in the entertainment industry.

"I saw Tyler again today."

Lindsey gasped. "Really? So he finally called?"

Sissy hummed. "Um, not exactly. But that's not the point." She'd waited almost two full days before breaking down and texting him. The method she'd used to facilitate their second meeting wasn't important.

"You're going to scare him away!" Lindsey exclaimed.

"I'm being careful."

Lindsey had been there for Sissy through everything—when her dad died, when she moved to Atlanta, and also when she'd had a child's crush on Tyler Hart.

Some things didn't change. Lindsey's friendship was one of them, and Sissy's crush on Tyler was another.

"I just worry about you..." Lindsey said, trailing off at the end.

"I'm fine. It's just fun." Most everything was *just fun* to Sissy, but there was suddenly pressure to have fun with Tyler. She wanted it to work out. She wanted him to have fun with her. She'd never cared about things like that before, and she wasn't sure why it mattered so much with Tyler.

Lindsey was silent for a moment. "I know you, Sis."

Her best friend could see through her toughest facade. Sissy sighed, caught in the act. "Yeah, I know, me too."

The phone vibrated in Sissy's hand, and she held it out to see who was calling. Dakota.

"Hey, I need to run, but I'll call you back later."

"That's okay. I wasn't calling for anything important," Lindsey said. "I was just thinking about you."

"Thanks, friend. Love you."

"Love you too."

Sissy switched to Dakota's call. "Hey there."

"Sis."

That one timid word said more than a thousand, and while her brother called her most days, he was in a dark place when he called today. She could always tell by his greeting if he'd been thinking about losing Lindsey.

She got to her knees beside the bed and pulled a duffel bag from beneath it. "I can be there in an hour. Want me to bring a pizza?"

When Dakota called, she came running. She'd left friends, dates, and classes to rush to her brother when he needed her. He had a handful of friends he could call, but there was a reason why he chose to call *her*. She was the one who never ran out of things to talk about, and her incessant ramblings kept his mind off Lindsey.

If it kept him from falling into depression, she'd be there for him the rest of her life.

"Sounds good. Get the garlic sauce."

Sissy stuffed clothes into the duffel along with her toiletry bag that stayed packed and ready. She'd bunk at her mom's and head back early to watch the Wilson kids in the morning.

"Got it. Be there soon."

"Thanks, Sis."

She knew what it cost him every time he thanked her for running to his rescue. They'd talked about his struggles at length, and he was ashamed to let anyone know his weakness—except her.

"Anytime." She hung up the phone and headed for the door. She doubled back and grabbed a deck of cards out of a junk drawer in the kitchen. It had been a while since she'd played a game with Dakota.

On the dark drive from Atlanta to Carson, Taylor Swift kept Sissy in good company. She skipped over the sappy songs and turned up the volume to sing along with the upbeat tunes. If she was walking into Dakota's house, she needed to be in her most positive headspace.

Rain pelted the windshield as her car jerked up Dakota's muddy drive. He'd just finished building the house, but the driveway and landscaping would come later. She admired her brother's handiwork. Actually, they'd made it a team effort. He could build a frame, but the poor guy didn't know the color coral from salmon. Thankfully, he had Sissy and her design skills to keep him on track.

She grabbed a ring of color swatches and the pizza before pulling up her hood and running through the pouring rain. She darted inside and slipped out of her raincoat before she dripped water all over the cheap rug. She hadn't found the perfect fit for the entryway yet, so this one would have to do.

Dakota appeared from the kitchen. "I wouldn't have asked you to come if I'd known it would be raining like this."

Her hair had air dried on the way over, and she

shook it out before pulling it into a top bun. "Technically, you didn't ask, and you can't change the weather, so here I am."

He grabbed the paper plates while she tossed the pizza onto the table. Well, Dakota didn't have a real table. He'd been using a thick piece of plywood attached to some two-by-fours as a makeshift table since he moved in.

"When are you gonna finish up the table?" she asked as she grabbed the napkins.

"It's finished. I just need help moving it over here."

"Count me out."

"I didn't ask you. I don't need your noodle arms."

"Hey, these noodle arms can throw a softball at sixty miles an hour." She kissed her bicep for emphasis.

"Softball. You said softball like it was the same as baseball." Dakota bit off half the pizza slice and shook his head.

Sissy held up a finger. "Stop right there."

Dakota's phone rang, and he fished it out of his pocket. "Hello."

Sissy took the opportunity to eat a slice of pizza. She intended to fill up on pepperoni, cheese, and black olives before she showed Dakota how to lose at five card.

"No problem," Dakota said to the person on the other end of the call. "I just wanted to see if you're plannin' on making your way up here this weekend. I need a set of hands moving the new table to the house."

Sissy swallowed a bite and mouthed, "Brian?"

Dakota shook his head and mouthed back, "Tyler."

Sissy shoved another hunk of pizza into her mouth to hide her reaction. She wasn't sure why her heart rate sped every time she heard his name, but she liked it.

"No, it's all right. Sissy's here. I'll just ask Brian or Jake to give me a hand."

Now she was wondering what Tyler was up to besides dodging her brother's calls. Had Dakota called him while they were at the lake earlier? And what plans did he have this weekend? She guzzled a bottle of water while she turned her ear to their conversation.

"Nah, man. Don't make a special trip. I can get anybody to help. I was really hopin' we could hit the lake after."

The water in Sissy's throat bubbled and she choked. Did Dakota know about the dip she and Tyler had taken earlier? Surely not.

"Okay. Meet at my place around nine on Saturday morning. See ya."

Dakota tossed his phone onto the table and picked up the slice of pizza on his plate. "You brought color swatches? Are you gonna make me work tonight?" he whined.

"As if you've done any of the decorating so far. Just leave it to the expert." She wiped her hands on a napkin, feeling sure that her overly-protective brother had no idea she'd almost kissed his friend a few hours ago.

Had she really almost kissed Tyler Hart? Her mouth tugged out at the corners when she remembered the way his strong arms had held her close in the warm water.

"Why are you smilin' like that? You look goofy," Dakota teased.

She picked up a stray olive from her plate and threw it at him. She felt a lot better when it hit his forehead and fell into his lap.

"You're so mature," he responded.

"I know you are, but what am I?" She couldn't contain her chuckle. "Sorry, but you asked for that one."

Dakota rolled his eyes. "Where are the cards?"

She pulled them out of the pocket of her sweatpants. "One rule: No cheesy chips around my brand new cards."

"Well, that doesn't sound like fun," Dakota said as he grabbed the deck.

Sissy pushed back her chair and picked up both empty plates to toss in the trash. "It sounds like I'll get to use this new pack of cards more than once, which was my intention when I bought them. Yours are always nasty." She shuddered at the thought of the sticky smears on the last deck of cards she'd found at his house.

Dakota rolled his eyes. "Fine. I'll call Brian next time."

"Good for you. You might actually win for once."

Dakota pulled the cards from the new box and slapped the deck on the table. "Whatever. Just deal."

She was thankful Dakota had called. If he hadn't, she'd have sat around wondering what Tyler had thought about ending up in the lake.

Too bad playing poker with her brother wasn't keeping her mind occupied nearly as much as she'd hoped. She was losing almost every hand because her heart wasn't in the game.

After a few hours and switching from five card to hold 'em, Dakota leaned back in his chair. "You should probably call it a night. That's the seventh game in a row you've lost."

Sissy stretched her neck. Her eyelids felt heavy as she shuffled the deck. "Yeah. I know when to walk away and when to run."

"You goin' to Mom's?" he asked.

"Yeah. I have to be back in the morning to keep the kids, so I better get to bed."

Dakota rubbed the back of his neck. "Thanks for comin'. I got off work early, and when I sit here..." He crossed his arms and scanned the unfinished room. The house was built, but the inside still needed a lot of work. "I just think too much."

Sissy lazily stretched her smile. "I know."

She knew he'd bought this land for Lindsey. She knew he'd planned to propose the last time he flew to New York to visit her. And she knew that he'd spent the last few years building a house for a wife he'd never have.

"Go to bed," Sissy said as she stuffed the cards back in the box and into her pocket. "I'm taking the leftover pizza for breakfast."

"Sorry," Dakota said, wincing.

"You ate it all?"

Dakota held his hands out. "You went to the bathroom, and I was still hungry."

She slammed the empty box closed. "You're a pig. You stuffed two slices of pizza in your mouth while I was gone. Shame on you."

He grabbed his wallet from the counter and pulled out a bill. "Here."

"I don't want your apology money. I'm getting two pizzas next time."

Dakota perked up. "That sounds like a good idea."

"Ugh. You're impossible." She walked out the door as Dakota chuckled behind her. She was leaving her brother in a better mood than when he called her earlier, and her work was finished here.

CHAPTER 8

Tyler

Tyler had made a point to be on his best behavior all week, but Lisa still watched him like a hawk. She was ready to die on that hill.

He couldn't take much credit for his improved attitude. Dr. Wilson had been right. Sissy was good for him, but he wasn't ready to admit it just yet.

He thought about Sissy's bubbly demeanor and impulsive sweetness before he entered each exam room, and it had done wonders for his rapport with the patients.

Apparently, thinking of Sissy made him happy. Shocker.

On the flip side, thinking of Sissy made him confused. He hadn't texted her or called her all week. He *wanted* to call her, but he also knew it was risky to give her more of his headspace than she already occupied.

Sissy could potentially rule his thoughts, and that

was scary. She was all-consuming, and it would be so easy to let her take over.

Dr. Wilson stepped out of her office as he passed. She was holding one of the tablets they used for record keeping, but she stopped and pulled it to her chest when she saw him. "Oh, just the person I wanted to see. The week is almost over, and I've noticed a marked difference in your demeanor."

Tyler nodded with a grin. "You can say you told me so."

"Do you understand why I'm glad I was right?" she asked.

"I do, and I appreciate your advice." He was still waffling over his thoughts about Sissy, but it was clear her brightness had rubbed off on him. Moments like this made him want to give in to the crushing impulse to call her.

Doctor Wilson excused herself, and Tyler continued to his office. The clinic was closing, and he needed to decide if he was going to Carson this evening or tomorrow. He was helping Dakota move the table in the morning, so it would probably be better to go on tonight.

Thoughts of Dakota would always interrupt any pleasant thoughts about Sissy. As much as he wanted to give in to the urge to pursue something with her, she'd always been off-limits. Tyler wasn't sure what Dakota would think if he mentioned his interest in Sissy, but he didn't have much hope for a blessing.

Tyler had just cleared off his desk when a text came through on his phone.

Sissy: One word?

Tyler rubbed his forehead. If she was trying to shake his resolve, her plan was working. Had she been fighting the urge to contact him all week the way he had done?

She wanted one word, but a dozen different words coursed through his thoughts when he looked at Sissy's text.

Tyler: Guilty.

He could have gone with "confused," but that was a little more than he was willing to share at this point. Guilty was something she would understand.

He laid the phone down, and it dinged immediately.

Sissy: Is this about Dakota?

Of course it was about Dakota. And their differences. And their ages. But he decided to focus on one obstacle at a time.

Sissy: Because this isn't your fault.

No, Dakota's depression after Lindsey left him wasn't Tyler's fault, but it was his responsibility to be available if his friend needed him.

Tyler: He called me. I didn't answer.

He should have just answered the phone Monday night instead of chickening out. Dakota had called Sissy next, and she'd driven an hour back to Carson after dark. That should have been Tyler going out of his way to help his friend.

Sissy: This is his problem, not yours. None of us can save him. He has to do it himself.

It was the truth, but it didn't make him feel any less responsible for Sissy having to go out of her way.

Tyler was tired of Sissy always saying the right things and making everything seem okay. Did she have this effect on everyone, or was he just conveniently blinded by her ability to wash away his guilt?

Tyler: He wouldn't approve.

There. That was a truth she couldn't deny.

Sissy: Yes he would. Plus, it's none of his business.

Tyler: He has enough going on. Telling him about us would only make things worse.

He put the phone down and propped his elbows on the desk and rested his head in his hands. How had Sissy thrown his whole world into chaos in such a short time? She had him questioning everything.

His phone dinged and he glanced at the lit-up screen.

Sissy: So there's an us?

No, there wasn't an us. There shouldn't be an us.

But he wanted it. He wanted her. He wanted her light and her happiness and the way she looked at him. He wanted her sweet words that seemed to always point out the bright side.

His realization came crashing forward. He was completely hung up on Sissy Calhoun, and he had no idea how it had happened.

Needing a minute, he gathered his things and

locked up his office. On the way out of the clinic he texted Sissy.

Tyler: Driving.

That would give him time to process his thoughts. The drive home was short, but he could mull everything over while he wasn't looking at her name on his phone screen.

When he pulled up at his place, he shut off the truck and looked at his phone in the passenger seat. This was it. If he opened up to her and gave any indication that they could move forward, there was no going back.

There were two texts waiting from Sissy.

Sissy: I know it hasn't been long since we met for dinner, but I won't hide how I feel. I hope there's an us or at least a chance to find out.

Sissy: Dakota tries to look out for me, but he's not my dad.

Tyler hung his head. Sissy's dad died when she was young, and the mess she was dealing with from Dakota wasn't a walk in the park. His chest hurt just thinking about a joyful person like Sissy dealing with the loss of someone she loved.

Tyler: I'm sorry about your dad.

He wasn't sure if he'd ever said those words to her before. He probably hadn't, but he definitely meant them now, and he needed to say it. Sissy's kindness and selflessness came from both parents. Tyler was old enough to recall many memories of her dad. He'd been a respected man in Carson.

He still hadn't gotten out of the truck when his phone dinged again.

Sissy: Give me one word. Make it a good one.

Feeling like he was somehow responsible for leading her to memories of her dad, he thought hard before responding.

Tyler: Lake.

It was his turn to make a move, and he wanted it to be a good one.

Sissy: Which one?

Tyler: I'll pick you up.

He got out of the truck and ran inside to change clothes and grab some rods and a tackle box. Minutes later, he was back in the truck and checking a text from Sissy where she'd given her address. He plugged it into the GPS. Thirty minutes later, he was pulling into the drive of an older house in a quiet neighborhood. He parked behind Sissy's purple car and got out. He hadn't thought to wonder where Sissy lived while she was in college, but he expected something more imposing. The quaint neighborhood was much more subdued than Sissy's larger-than-life personality.

Sissy met him at the door with her greeting smile. It was the one where her brown eyes darkened as her pupils dilated—one of the many smiles he'd chronicled in the last week.

"Hey."

"Ready?" he asked.

She looped her arm in his and practically dragged

him to the truck. He opened the passenger door for her, and she gave him a sweet smile as she climbed in.

He walked around to the driver's side, and Sissy was talking before he opened the door.

"I'm so excited! Where are we going?"

Tyler started the truck, already feeling lighter knowing Sissy was happy. "I was thinking Bridge Stone Lake." They had a few hours before the sun went down. "You want to grab something quick for dinner before we go?"

"Yeah. Can we have a picnic at the lake?"

The mosquitos were going to eat them alive, but he suddenly felt like being insect food if Sissy got what she wanted. "Sure. Sandwiches from Salvatore's?"

Sissy laid a hand on his arm as he backed out of the drive. "It's like you read my mind."

It was going to be a long evening if Sissy kept casually touching him. He was already overwhelmed by the pressure to show her a good time, and he didn't have any headspace left to analyze the way her skin felt against his.

She called in a pickup order as soon as they were on the road. At Salvatore's, Tyler offered to run in and grab the sandwiches, but Sissy caught up to him at the door and plastered herself to his side.

They waited two excruciating minutes for the sandwiches to be ready. Tyler knew because he counted every second Sissy held onto his arm. With both of her arms wrapped around his and her excited smile looking up at him, two minutes felt like plenty of time to work himself up to stroke level blood pressure.

Back in the truck with sandwiches in tow, Sissy talked about the places she missed in Carson that included The Line and Jojo's.

Bridge Stone Lake was enclosed in a private neighborhood suburb, but Tyler had plenty of friends who lived here and granted him full access to their docks. He texted his friend, Josh, earlier, letting him know he'd be coming by to fish.

"Wow, this place is adorable!" Sissy looked out each window in turn, checking out the scenery.

Tyler pulled into the drive of a single-level house and parked the truck. Flowers and greenery overfilled the yard, but Sissy's attention was focused on the quiet lake across the road.

"Can you grab the food?" Tyler asked as he picked up the fishing rods and tackle box.

When they started across the road, Sissy plastered herself to his side again. She was like a magnet, and he was her counterpart.

And suddenly, the old opposites attract adage made sense, at least while Sissy was pinned to his side.

Tyler put the rods and tackle box in the rowboat tied to the dock before reaching for the bag of sandwiches Sissy carried. He'd stepped into this boat dozens of times, but today felt something like preparing for battle.

Entertainment? Check.

Sustenance? Check.

Mission plan? To be determined.

Stakes? High.

With one foot in the bottom of the boat and one on the dock, Tyler offered Sissy a helping hand.

She accepted it and gave him a sweet smile that said she was impressed. "Thank you."

That was a new smile to add to his list, and it was his favorite so far. He made a mental note to do every gentlemanly thing he'd ever heard of while Sissy was around.

She settled onto the middle bench, and Tyler took his place on the back bench facing her. He slid the tackle box beneath his seat and secured the rods to the side before pulling out the oars.

Sissy didn't speak as he rowed them past the end of the dock and turned to follow the shore to the east. If he wanted Sissy to have a good time, he'd have to reveal his biggest secret: the sweet spot.

Every body of water with fish in it had one. Bigger lakes had hundreds. But this private lake was small enough that motorized vehicles were prohibited, and he'd found a brush pile years ago that was guaranteed to have fish in it. Bass were spawning right now, and he wanted Sissy to experience the small victories of catching fish.

When they reached the spot, Tyler anchored the boat and pulled out the sandwiches and two small bottles of water.

"It's beautiful here," Sissy said as she looked from one side to the other.

Tyler handed her a sandwich. "It is. I thought about buying a place out here." He shrugged. "Maybe one day."

Sissy was lifting the sandwich to her mouth when she stopped. "So, you have a five-year plan?"

"Mostly. Finish my residency. Get a job at a family clinic." He stopped before admitting that finding a woman to spend the rest of his life with was on that list too. "What about you?"

"I don't have a plan. I'd like to finish college and have a family, but…" She tucked her chin and took another bite of the sandwich.

Sissy's dating history was something he desperately wanted to know more about. Why hadn't some lucky guy tried to get her to settle down?

And that was the crux. Sissy wasn't the settling down type. She was full speed ahead in whichever way the wind blew her.

Tyler finished his sandwich before Sissy, and he pulled the tackle box from beneath the bench seat. Sissy watched silently, and he wasn't sure if that was a good thing or a bad thing. He'd only ever known Sissy to talk his head off, and the silence had him concerned. She didn't say a word, even after she crumpled the sandwich wrapper and stashed it in the trash bag.

Remembering his purpose to cheer her up, he opened a bag of worms and tossed one into her lap. As he'd expected, she jumped and squealed.

He chuckled as he kept his attention on the lure he was attaching to a hook, and he wasn't prepared when

Sissy reached over the side of the boat and flung a handful of water at him.

"Hey!" he said, shaking the drops from his hair. "I want to stay moderately dry on this trip." He pointed a scolding finger at her.

She bit her lips between her teeth to stifle a laugh and crossed her heart with a finger.

That was better. The sadness in Sissy's tone earlier had shaken him up. It was all wrong and didn't belong to Sissy. She was meant to be carefree and happy.

"What do you know about fishing?" he asked.

"You put a dangling something on a hook on the end of the line and throw it out in the water." She flung her arm out to point out the wide-open lake. "Then you reel it in. Odds of successfully catching a fish on that line seem to be low, considering what I've seen from you and Dakota over the years."

Tyler straightened his shoulders. "That's not true!"

Sissy contemplated his response before saying, "No, I think that's about right. You spend more time hanging out and chitchatting than actually fishing."

"That's not true either. We hardly ever talk, and that's why Dakota and I make great fishing partners."

Sissy threw her head back in exasperation. "So, I'm not allowed to talk?"

"Actually, I *want* you to talk." If talking made Sissy happy, he'd listen to her all evening.

"In that case, I'll forgo the rod and just relax." She tucked her hands under her thighs and looked out over the lake.

Tyler shrugged, hoping he hadn't screwed up the date by taking her to do something she didn't enjoy.

Ugh. When had he started thinking of it as a date?

It didn't matter when. What mattered was that he was thinking of Sissy more often, and he was beginning to protect the time he got to spend with her.

Tyler cast his rod toward the bank. "What's your favorite thing to do?"

When Sissy didn't answer right away, he turned to see her dark eyes trained on him. The gentle upturn of her smile had his breaths coming faster and his mouth going dry.

Being with Sissy gave him a slight thrill that he hadn't experienced until now, and he was quickly becoming addicted to the excitement she stirred inside of him.

"I like babysitting," she said.

"Like, watching other people's kids?"

Sissy giggled. "Yes! Well, not watching them in a creepy way like you make it sound. I like hanging out with kids. They're fun, and they're usually happy."

Tyler reeled in his lure and made another cast just left of the first. "You babysit Dr. Wilson's kids?"

"Yep. Almost every evening." Sissy leaned back to look at the clouds. "After being with adults and teenagers at school all day, it's nice to relax."

Tyler made a humph sound in his chest. "Kids are *not* relaxing."

"Not like sit on the couch and read relaxing, but I don't have to be rigid or proper or any of the other things adults expect. I can just have fun and be myself."

And it all made sense. Sissy was inherently joyful, and she felt most at home with people who brought out that happiness in herself—kids.

Sissy continued, speaking a little faster in her excitement. "Like the other day, Marie and David were shopping for a new car, and Claire prayed they would choose a purple one like mine. I didn't have the heart to tell her it wasn't even a possibility."

She continued to laugh at the memory, and Tyler felt his chest swelling, expanding to breathe in the joy she radiated.

Tyler felt a tug on his line and set the hook. As he reeled faster, then slower so the line wouldn't break when the fish darted away from him in the water, Sissy leaned closer.

"You got one?" she asked, excitement heavy in her tone.

"Yep." He reeled faster again and pulled against the bowing rod. "It's a big one."

When the fish jumped out of the water closer to the canoe, he saw that it *was* a big one. Probably the largest he'd caught all spring.

Sissy laughed when the largemouth bass slung water her way with a flip of its tail. "He's a fighter."

Tyler reached into the water and grabbed the fish by the lip. When he lifted it from the water, it thrashed, spraying Sissy with more drops.

She bounced in excitement, causing the rowboat to

rock. They both quickly sat on the benches to center the weight and keep from losing their balance.

A surge of something euphoric swelled in Tyler's chest, bubbling up and bursting out in a riotous laugh.

Sissy cupped her cheeks and continued to laugh. "Look at you! You look so happy!"

He stopped laughing, but a wide grin remained on his face. "I am."

It was the truth and a realization. He'd always thought fishing was relaxing, but this was fun. It was a new level of enjoyment doing the same thing he'd been doing his whole life.

He'd been doing it wrong. The key was Sissy—in fishing and his life. She was the key to happiness.

Sissy waved her hands. "Do it again."

Tyler shook his head, still smiling. "I've never seen anyone so excited over a fish." He pulled the hook out of the fish's lip and tossed it back into the water.

"If you don't have fun fishing, why do you do it?" she asked.

Tyler shrugged as he fixed his worm on the hook. "It's peaceful. I don't have to worry about moving patients through the clinic or dictating records or any of the important things that I do every day."

Sissy propped her elbows on her knees, leaning forward as if she were hanging on his every word. "Do you like being a doctor?"

"Yes, it's what I've always wanted to do. I never considered anything else."

Sissy hummed. "Professional fisherman wasn't a contender?"

Tyler laughed. "Nope. I like things I can count on. I like stability."

He snuck a glance at her and found her looking back at him. Sissy was the opposite of stability, but she was dependable. She'd leave on a moment's notice to help her brother. Dr. Wilson trusted Sissy to take care of her kids.

How could he both love and dislike two key parts of her? She continued to confuse him at every turn.

They sat in silence as the light began to dim. Not from the coming dusk, but a thick, gray cloud was moving in from the west.

"We should probably go. I didn't check the weather before we left," Tyler admitted. He didn't really care about the forecast. Right now, he'd rather be safe than sorry he'd been caught out on the lake during a lightning storm.

Sissy tapped away on her phone as he stored his rod and grabbed the oars.

"It looks like a popup thunderstorm. The forecast doesn't say much about it."

He rowed toward his friend's dock much faster than he'd rowed out onto the lake. Sissy was probably right about a popup thunderstorm. Georgia springs and summers were notorious for ten-minute showers.

The warm air had grown thick and humid by the time he pulled the boat up to the dock and held it secure so Sissy could step out. He pulled the keys from his pocket and handed them to her. "You can go on to the truck. I wouldn't want you to get wet."

She took the keys and grabbed their trash bag, stowing it in the covered trash bin secured to the dock near the bank.

Tyler pulled the boat onto the dock. He'd really hoped to stay dry on this outing, but he was still securing the ropes around the boat when tiny drops started hitting the top of his head and landing on his arms as he worked.

The rain picked up as he grabbed the rods and tackle box to make a run for the truck, but Sissy was standing on the bank not two steps from the dock.

"What are you doing?" he yelled as he marched toward her, intent on ushering her toward the truck. The looney toon was just standing there like she didn't care that it was raining.

Granted, Sissy probably didn't care. She didn't care about anything.

She didn't move as he reached her and gestured toward the truck with the rods in his hand. "Sissy—"

She threw her arms around him, and her lips landed on his. He inhaled one deep breath full of sunshine before he disentangled himself from her.

Stepping back, something between irritation and exhilaration surged within him. "What are you doing?" His tone was too high, and this was uncharted territory. His head was so full of Sissy that he couldn't think straight.

She looked up at him, and he knew he'd lost the

battle—the one he'd been fighting with himself. She was the one he should stay away from, but she was the one he wanted. They were all wrong for each other, but being with Sissy felt more right than anything else.

Finally giving in to his desires, he dropped the tackle box and rods and closed the distance. His hands cupped her face and slid into her hair.

"You're so stubborn," Tyler breathed. "Stop stealing my thunder and let me kiss you first."

Then he kissed her, crashing his mouth into hers with a force that the sky echoed in thunder.

CHAPTER 9
Sissy

The boom in the air vibrated over Sissy's skin, but it didn't touch the earth-shattering force of the man in her arms.

She grabbed his shoulders, trying to pull him closer when there wasn't any room left between them. He tightened his hold, as if the current of wind and rain might wash them away from each other.

She felt it too—the rush to erase the space they'd been fighting against. She hadn't meant to actually do it, but in the moment, she'd been compelled to kiss him.

His fingers curled into her hair as he drank her in, every inch of her skin zinged as the fire in his kiss matched hers.

She was pushing, but he wasn't backing up this time. The calculating doctor had thrown all of his excuses to the wind. He was kissing her as if the movement of his mouth against hers could sustain him.

The rain was falling harder, dripping from her hair and down her face, but she couldn't bring herself to care. Her world had just shifted, and Tyler was all that mattered right now. The sweet man had brought her to a beautiful lake to cheer her up, and he'd done more than that. He'd opened up to her and laughed. It was a sound she'd never forget.

Thunder rolled around them, and the lingering echoes were strong enough to pull them out of the kiss.

Tyler looked out over the lake. He was breathing hard and still cradling her face, though much more gently now.

He turned his attention back to her, still unmoving in the pouring rain. "We'd better go."

He grabbed the rods and tackle box, and she followed him up the slight hill and across the road to the driveway where they'd parked his truck. He threw the tackle box in the bed of the pickup truck before opening the passenger side door for her to climb in. She was dripping wet, and she paused. She hated to get the inside of his truck wet knowing he wouldn't like it.

Tyler jerked his head toward the cab. "It's fine."

Lightning crashed nearby, and Sissy yelped. A strike that loud had to have struck something.

"Get in," Tyler commanded, cutting another glance at the darkening sky.

Well, that was pretty clear. It wasn't as if they had much choice but to climb inside soaking wet.

Once she was settled in the seat, Tyler closed the

door and rounded the truck. He jumped in the driver's side and closed the door behind him. Torrential rain was pelting the roof, but the noise was muffled inside the cab.

Tyler turned to her, and that heart-stopping smile greeted her like a rainbow after the storm. It made her heart feel light enough to float.

Without warning, he shook his head, slinging water from his hair all over her and the interior of the truck.

"Eww! Stop!" she screamed, but her laughter drowned out any real protest in her words.

She'd had her suspicions that Tyler was a fun guy under his stuffy doctor's coat, but this was better than she'd ever dreamed.

His smile would have lingered if he hadn't bitten his lower lip to hide it. She knew because his eyes were still smiling. Yes, eyes could smile, and Tyler's were gloriously bright.

Her attention fell to his mouth, and she remembered the way he'd captivated her when they'd kissed.

And oh, boy. This doctor could kiss. He'd been holding onto her, but she could've sworn she'd been falling with nowhere to land. It was that sinking feeling where her stomach felt like it was falling when the roller coaster dives from the highest peak.

"One word?" Sissy asked in a whisper. Every inch of her body was on high alert, pulled tight in anticipation, and she had to know what he was thinking right now. Was he feeling what she was feeling?

His breathing was still deep and quick, and his gaze darted to her mouth and back to her eyes. "Terrified."

Oh, that was a big word. A word that had significance and the power to change everything. Fear and love were the most powerful emotions.

"One from you too," he said.

She thought for a moment before speaking the word on her heart. "Happy."

It was too fast. Too much. And Tyler was the kind that scared easily. She knew it because she'd been putting people off with her excitability and impulsive nature her whole life. She had to walk a thin line, or she could lose him.

He leaned toward her, and her pulse rate climbed. But instead of kissing her, he gently brushed a hand over her cheek and rested his forehead against hers as he whispered, "Time."

Another powerful word. Time could mean so many things, but she knew Tyler needed space to wrap his head around the shift in their relationship. It was big enough to cause Sissy to pause and step back, and that meant it was monumental enough that slowing down to figure everything out was probably a good idea. It wasn't something she did often—stop to think before she acted—but Tyler was rubbing off on her in a good way.

"If you need time to overthink it, I guess I can let you do that," Sissy said with a chuckle. She wanted to lighten the mood before he took her home.

Sissy's phone rang in her pocket, breaking the tension of the moment. "It's Marie Wilson."

She answered quickly. "Hello."

"Sissy, are you busy? Cody fell into the edge of the dresser in his bedroom and split his brow open. He needs stitches."

Sissy's hand flew to her cheek. Hearing about Cody's injury made her stomach roll. "Is he okay?"

"He'll be fine, but I need to take him to Children's Hospital, and I really don't want to bring the other kids with me. Claire is already in bed."

"Hold on," Sissy said as she pulled the phone from her ear to type in the Wilsons' address. She put the phone back to her ear. "I can be there in twenty minutes."

"Are you sure? I hate to bother you this late on a Friday night, but David is out of town, and the neighbors are elderly. I'd hate to ask them to get out."

"No problem at all. I'm on my way."

"Thank you," Marie breathed. "Be careful."

"I will. Be there soon."

Sissy disconnected the call and turned to Tyler. "Can you take me to Dr. Wilson's house? She needs to take one of her kids to the hospital, and she wants me to watch the other two."

Tyler started the truck. "Tell me where to go. Do you want me to swing by your place so you can get some things?"

Sissy shook her head. "It's too far out of the way, and she said it's a head wound. I'd feel much better if they got there quickly. I'll text Christy and ask her to meet me there with some dry clothes." She inhaled sharply. Why was she losing her breath as if she'd been running?

Tyler pulled out onto the residential road leading out of the neighborhood. He reached over to put his strong hand on hers. "Hey, everything is going to be fine. We'll be there soon."

Sissy's breathing was still deep, and her nerves were shot. Hearing about poor Cody getting hurt had really shaken her up, and for once, she didn't have all the words. She whispered, "I know," and that was enough.

CHAPTER 10
Tyler

Tyler pulled up at Dakota's house just before nine the next morning. The summer sun was already warm. It looked as if they wouldn't have to battle the weather today.

Dakota had just finished building the house, but the driveway was still riddled with potholes and washed-out crevices. The storm must have come through Carson last night too because the area in front of the house was a muddy disaster.

Tyler parked off to the side to keep the front entrance clear for unloading. An old, olive-green, flatbed truck was parked in front of the farmhouse, and he grabbed a pair of work gloves from the console before getting out to inspect the vehicle. Thankfully, it had a motorized lift gate that would make moving the table a piece of cake.

He stepped up on the porch and admired the view. Dakota had a nice one here—nothing but country in sight. Tyler didn't live in the most metropolitan part of Atlanta, but it also wasn't *this*. If given the choice, he'd pick the quiet, simple life of a small town any day.

Dakota's front door was painted cerulean blue and stood out against the light exterior. For the first time, Tyler recognized Sissy's hand in this place. He knew she was an interior designer, but he'd never thought about what she actually *did* with that talent.

Apparently, she made ordinary colors into something captivating because that door was impossible to miss.

Tyler didn't bother knocking. He stepped inside and looked around. The lights were off, and everything was quiet.

He knocked on the doorframe and called out, "Dakota." When no one answered, Tyler figured he must have gone on over to the barn.

Tyler turned to leave and grabbed the doorknob just as Dakota yelled, "Just a second!" from down the hallway.

Stepping into the kitchen, Tyler intended to help himself to a drink, but the fridge was close to empty. There was mustard, ketchup, pickles, and orange juice but not a bottle of water in sight.

There were a few inches of coffee left in the pot, so he grabbed a mug from the cabinet and filled it half full. He might not have time to drink the whole cup.

He lifted the mug to his lips, but quickly began spitting and sputtering when the liquid hit his mouth. It was cold and tasted like dirt.

After wiping his mouth, he smelled the coffee. It even smelled wrong. There wasn't any of that magic bean smell that fueled his mornings.

Dakota barged into the kitchen still buckling his belt. He didn't so much as glance Tyler's way as he said, "Sorry. I overslept."

Tyler checked the clock on the microwave. "It's nine in the morning. You never sleep past six."

Dakota rubbed the back of his neck as he looked around the room. "Have you seen my boots?"

Tyler raised a brow. "No. I'm not your mommy." He held up the mug of slush. "What is this junk?"

Dakota's eyes widened. "Um. Don't drink that."

"Yeah, I got that memo. A little late. What's your problem?" Tyler recognized his signature brusk tone, but Dakota wasn't a patient, and no one here was going to complain to his boss.

Dakota looked everywhere but at Tyler. The guy was hiding something, and his face looked slightly pale. Was he sweating?

Tyler sloshed the toxic muck into the sink. "Dude, spill it."

Dakota spotted his boots by the back door and darted for them like they were a lifeline.

Tyler leaned back against the counter and crossed his arms over his chest. He wasn't leaving here until he figured out what was going on.

With his boots on, Dakota stood and grabbed his phone from the counter. "Ready?"

"Not a chance. Start talking," Tyler firmly said.

Dakota opened his arms and held his hands out, palms up. "Nothing is up."

"Lie. Try again."

Dakota slowly shook his head and looked away. "I can't keep living like this."

"Like what?" Tyler asked.

"Without... her."

Tyler rubbed his jaw. Lindsey had been gone for a while, but Dakota hadn't made it to the acceptance stage yet. "I get it, but don't you think it's time to move on?"

Dakota huffed. "Did you spend your whole life with the woman you thought would be your wife one day and then lose her?" Dakota's volume rose with every word.

Tyler shook his head.

"No! You haven't!" Dakota yelled. "It's not fair. Lindsey was my life, and I'm lost without her."

"Hey, chill out," Tyler urged. He walked across the kitchen, intending to give his friend an encouraging pat on the shoulder, but something else caught his attention when he got close.

Tyler tightened the hand he'd been intending to slap on Dakota's shoulder into a fist. "Are you drunk?"

Dakota's eyes were red around the dark-brown irises as he met Tyler's stare. "I messed up the best thing in my life."

"Are you drunk?" Tyler asked again, enunciating each word.

Dakota rubbed a hand over his mouth before

answering, "Yes. Okay. I drank. I drink." He huffed. "A lot. It's the only thing that helps me forget."

He was stumbling over his words as if he couldn't put the thought together. Dakota was normally intelligent and focused. Tyler hadn't seen his friend unsettled like this before. Sure, he'd been bemoaning the loss of his relationship with Lindsey since she left, but this was different.

"Drinking doesn't help you forget. It impairs your judgment, harms your body, and can be addicting." The latter part scared Tyler the most. Was Dakota already too far into this problem? Whatever the case, he had to get a handle on it quickly.

"Does Sissy know about this?" Tyler questioned.

Dakota's brow furrowed. "What? No. Well, not really. But I'm not telling her. She knows I drink sometimes, but she doesn't know about" —Dakota threw his hand in the air— "This."

"You need to tell her." Tyler knew Sissy cared about her brother, and she would be there for him.

"No way. She'd lose her mind." Dakota rubbed his forehead. "Can you imagine? She'd gripe at me twenty-four-seven."

"And you'd deserve it. This isn't something to play around with. Are you missing work?"

Dakota's lips thinned. His delayed response was answer enough. Dakota took pride in his work, and missing had always been unacceptable.

"You've got to be kidding me!" Tyler yelled.

"You're gonna screw everything up if you don't get it together."

"I know. I know," Dakota conceded, holding up his hands in surrender. "I just... maybe I need help." He rubbed his forehead again, looking defeated.

"Is this why you called..." Tyler stopped just before he blurted out something he wasn't supposed to know—that Dakota had called Sissy last week, and she'd come running. "Is this why you called me last week?"

Dakota nodded. "Yeah."

Tyler sighed. Maybe Dakota didn't need the sharp reprimand he was getting. Maybe Tyler needed to calm down and be more understanding. That's what Sissy would do. She had more patience than anyone he knew. "Sorry, man. I didn't realize it was this serious."

"It's not," Dakota muttered, tucking his chin. "It's just easier not to think about Lindsey or drinking when someone else is around." He looked back up and stuck his hands in his pockets. "It's too quiet around here."

Tyler looked around, remembering the peacefulness he'd just admired about Dakota's place. Now he was considering it in light of Dakota's struggles.

"Have you talked to anyone about this?" Tyler asked, trying to regain some control over his temper and tone.

"No. Well, I talked to Declan a little."

"Declan isn't here," Tyler reminded him.

Dakota and Declan had been inseparable since they were kids, but Declan was stationed at Fort

Hood in Texas with the army and had been for a while. He wouldn't be much help if he wasn't around.

"I know." Dakota held up a hand and started ticking off the names of his friends. "Ian isn't here, Brian is busy, Jake is always on call, Marcus has his hands full with his brothers and sister, and you and Sissy live in Atlanta."

Tyler's shoulders tensed when he heard his and Sissy's names so close together. Why had it sounded like they were together?

Probably because they sort of *were* together.

"You know any of us will help you. If you sit around thinking about spiraling, call down your contact list until you find someone. And I'm sure Marcus could always use a hand with the kids. That would keep your mind busy."

"True. But I hate being so... weak." The last word was a quiet confession. "She was the best thing in my life."

"What about your family? What about Sissy? The Lord? All of those things should be the most important things in your life." Tyler huffed. "I can't say I know what you're going through, but you have a lot going for you, man. Don't throw that away."

"I'm not, but it's hard to keep going sometimes."

Tyler froze but tried not to draw attention to his reaction. Were things bad enough that his friend was ready to give up? For everyone's sake, he hoped Dakota hadn't chosen his words carefully.

"What about the house?" Tyler continued to grasp for possible solutions.

Dakota nodded. "It keeps my mind occupied, but it also reminds me of her. I did all this thinking I was investing in our future." He leaned back to rest against the wall. "I'm just tired."

Tyler tried to keep his expression composed while his friend used way too many phrases that sounded a lot like giving up. "We need to get you some help."

"I'm not ready for that," Dakota said.

"How are you not ready? You're falling into a trap if you think denial will fix your problems."

Dakota nodded but didn't speak as his gaze dropped to the floor.

"This is serious. You can't do this on your own," Tyler added.

"Well then help me, man." Dakota lifted his chin, but the words were pleading. "You're a professional. Let's just keep this between us, and you can keep me accountable."

"I'm not a professional secret keeper," Tyler said.

"Isn't that part of being a doctor?"

Tyler huffed. He wasn't a life coach, but people often tried to lump doctors into that group. "Not with friends. I'm not the kind of help you need. I think you should tell Sissy. She worries about you, and she cares. That's not a bad thing."

Dakota was already shaking his head. "I can't."

"You need all the help you can get," Tyler reminded him.

"She worries too much as it is. She'd be disappointed. And I'm her older brother. I'm supposed to be the one she can count on, not the other way around."

Tyler was shocked by Dakota's assessment of Sissy. Tyler had always thought Sissy didn't care about anything, but last night he'd witnessed her immediate response when Dr. Wilson needed help, and he knew she'd do anything for her brother.

"If you don't want Sissy to be disappointed in you, then get your act together."

Dakota dropped his head back against the wall. "That's why I'm telling you about this. Trust me. I didn't want to."

Tyler rubbed a hand through his hair and knew he'd regret this. "Okay. I'll help, but I can't run over here every evening to save you from yourself. I still think you need to talk to someone."

Dakota shook his head. "I just need someone to hold me accountable. I think that might help."

"So, I'm your babysitter?" Tyler said.

"Dude, you're the worst. I need a friend, not a drill sergeant."

Tyler sighed. The personality flaws that were getting him in trouble at work were revealing themselves this morning. "You're right. Sorry." He scratched his head. "Can you talk to one of the church counselors?"

"I can't. Mom works at the church."

"And would it be such a bad thing if your mom

knew? She could help you too. Your dad pastored that church most of his life. Your mom would know how to get you in touch with the people who could help."

Dakota shook his head. "No. I can't go to the church."

"That's their job. People go to them when they can't go anywhere else."

"Yeah, so I'm just supposed to stop by and say, 'Hey, I'm not being a very good Christian. Please help.'"

"Yes. That's exactly what you should do."

"People talk in this town," Dakota reminded him.

Tyler rolled his eyes. "Ms. Miller isn't a church employee. I think you're safe. We know those people, and they'll do anything to help you. Karen and Butch are both counselors. She was our teacher in middle school. She's great with those kinds of things."

Dakota stared at the floor as he contemplated. "I'm not ready for that yet."

"What about AA?"

"I don't want to talk to strangers about it. They don't know me."

"Maybe that's a good thing," Tyler pointed out. "You don't have to worry about what those people think. To be upfront, I'm not sure why you worry about what anyone you know thinks either. Addiction isn't something to mess around with."

"I'm not an addict. I'm just—"

Tyler held up a silencing hand. "I can't hear your

denial right now. Listen to me when I tell you that you need some help."

"Fine. I'll try a meeting."

"I'll send you the information on one in Atlanta. Then you won't bump into anyone you know."

"Thanks, man. I appreciate it. And please don't tell anyone."

Tyler hesitated. He didn't like keeping secrets, and he didn't like it one bit that Dakota wanted to keep this from Sissy. Maybe if he helped Dakota climb out of this mess, it wouldn't be an issue, and Sissy wouldn't have to worry. "Fine. But if I don't see improvement, we're gonna have to redefine the terms of this agreement."

Dakota pushed off the wall. "Fair enough."

"Before we move the table, I'm taking you to the grocery store. I need coffee, and you need to hydrate."

After they'd moved the table, Tyler and Dakota slipped out to the pond to cast a few lines. As usual, they didn't talk much, but Tyler felt their morning conversation hanging over them like a dark cloud, despite the warm, sunny day.

Wanting to keep a closer eye on his friend, Tyler invited Dakota to dinner at his parents' house. They wouldn't mind, and his mom cooked enough to feed the neighborhood every Saturday evening.

Tyler watched Dakota across the dinner table. He

was telling an animated story about Brian getting his shoelace caught in a weedeater, and Tyler was the only one at the table who wasn't laughing.

He wanted to laugh, especially at their friend's misfortunes. Brian was a jokester, and he loved to make people laugh, even at his own expense.

Tyler's mother wiped her eyes and continued to chuckle. "I don't know why anyone lets that boy run equipment."

"He's more capable than you'd think," his dad added, clearly defending his own decisions in hiring Brian to help fix things around the house. Tyler's dad was a capable man, but he watched his son's friends trying to make their place in the world, and he wanted to reward hard work and a job well done.

"You're right. I shouldn't give him such a hard time," Dakota admitted. "He's a good worker."

"I just hope Joe doesn't kick him off the job site before he figures out his way to a desk job," Tyler's dad said. "I wonder why he didn't follow his parents into the architectural field."

Dakota shrugged. "Beats me. He's on his third job this year. He needs to get somewhere and get settled soon."

Tyler watched and listened as Dakota and his parents talked. He seemed completely fine, and the realization that Dakota could hide the severity of his problem from anyone was terrifying.

When their plates were empty, and they'd talked through two rounds of sweet tea refills, they all stood.

Dakota rubbed the back of his neck and asked, "Can I help y'all clean up?"

Tyler's mom waved a hand. "Oh no. I'll take care of that."

Tyler jerked his head toward the kitchen. "No, ma'am. We're helping."

Dakota didn't hesitate to follow Tyler to the kitchen, despite his mother's continued assurance that she enjoyed cleaning up the kitchen. He imagined she liked it about as much as he enjoyed cutting grass. It was the one chore he always volunteered to do whenever he visited his parents. He'd been cutting the neighbor's grass since he was a kid.

Still, Tyler needed an excuse to keep his friend around as long as possible. If Dakota didn't spend as much time alone, maybe he wouldn't be tempted to drink and flush his future down the toilet.

When the kitchen was clean and Tyler's dad had explained the shelves he wanted Dakota's help building in the wood shed out back, he couldn't think of another reason to hinder his friend.

"Well, thanks again for dinner," Dakota said as he donned his Georgia Bulldogs baseball cap. "It was delicious as always."

"Thanks for coming. We'll see you next week." His mother waved.

"You bet. See ya." Dakota tipped his hat as he closed the door behind him.

Exhaustion settled on Tyler's shoulders. He'd

worried in silence most of the day, and he still wasn't sure he'd done enough.

"You okay?" his mom asked.

Tyler brushed a hand through his hair. "Yeah. I think I'm ready to hit the hay."

"I'm making bacon, biscuits, and gravy before church. See you in the morning."

Tyler nodded as he turned toward the stairs. "Good night."

"Ty."

He turned at his mother's call.

She looked up at him with a proud smile. "I'm glad you got to spend some time with Dakota today. He seems sad most days, but he was happy today."

Tyler tensed. How much did his parents know? Were there others who'd seen the change in his friend? "Me too."

"Good night," she called behind him.

Tyler stepped into his old bedroom and closed the door. His mother had converted it into a guest room when he moved out, but he and his grandparents were the only ones who used it.

Minutes later, he fell into bed and stared at the dark ceiling. Today hadn't been anything he'd expected, and he missed Sissy more than he'd anticipated.

When had she taken up residence in his head? He'd thought about her no less than ten times an hour, and Dakota's presence was an incessant reminder of the secret he'd promised to keep.

He grabbed his phone from the bedside table and texted her.

Tyler: One word?

Seconds later, she replied.

Sissy: Tired.

He'd barely read the message before the phone rang.

"Hello."

"Hey." The lazy tone of her voice confirmed her exhaustion. "I don't have the energy to text."

"Sorry to bother you. I just wanted to know how you were doing."

She sighed. "I didn't sleep much last night. I was too worked up waiting for Marie and Cody to get home."

Sissy had a heart like none he'd ever encountered. "Everything okay?"

"Yeah. He's fine. It just scared me. I hate the thought of one of these kids getting hurt." She paused a minute before whispering, "I love them so much."

Sissy was special. She wasn't like any woman he'd ever known. She loved without hesitation, with a love that was genuine and all-consuming.

"I know," Tyler said. "I'm glad he's okay. Those kids are lucky to have you."

Sissy chuckled, but the joyful sound was subdued. "I'm the lucky one."

Tyler swallowed hard and stared at the ray of moonlight shining through the window. If there was ever a time to tell her the truths he'd been trying to hide, it was now.

"I missed you today," he admitted, holding his breath for the unknown consequences of his honesty.

Her reply was easy and genuine. He could hear the truth in her words when she said, "I missed you more."

His chest ached, and his lungs labored to perform the simple task of breathing. Fear gripped his mind in a controlling vise.

He could easily get wrapped up in Sissy, but he feared she could leave him like Lindsey left Dakota. Tyler didn't want to picture his future being like Dakota—trudging through life like a ghost of the man he used to be.

Tyler knew he was in too deep to turn back now, but seeing Sissy and talking to her every day would make it difficult to keep Dakota's secret.

Was it really a bad thing that she cared too much and went out of her way for anyone who needed a hand?

Right now, he could see the toll it took on her to care so deeply. He could hear it in her voice. She gave so much of herself in service to others.

"Can I see you when I get back in town?" The words were out before he thought about them.

He was too far gone, and keeping her at a distance wasn't an option.

CHAPTER 11
Sissy

Sissy settled into her car and made a show of waving to the Wilson kids. Thankfully, her penchant for dramatic flair matched theirs, and they always gave her a big farewell when it was time to leave.

She loved those kids. Children weren't afraid to be open and honest, and it was a breath of fresh air not to have to worry about what they were thinking. They told her when they were angry, hugged her when they were happy, and cried when they were upset.

It didn't seem so difficult—being honest—but she knew first hand that not everyone shared that idea.

Thankfully, she had a circle of people she could trust—her mom, Lindsey, Christy, Dakota, Marie, and Tyler.

When she pulled into the driveway at her house, she remembered the lamps she'd ordered for Dakota's place were supposed to arrive today. She needed to check in on him anyway.

Holidays and summers were the worst for him since Lindsey left. Holidays were meant to be spent with the people you cared about, and the daylight lasted too long in the summers. He either worked himself to exhaustion or thought too much about the summers he'd spent with Lindsey.

Sissy missed her friend too, and she often had trouble keeping the two people in her life she loved most from crossing paths. Her brother and her best friend didn't live in the same world anymore.

She dialed his number as she got out of the car. The summer heat hit her like a wall of fire sucking the air from her lungs.

"Hello."

"Did you get a surprise today?" she asked.

"Um, no. What are you talking about?"

Sissy huffed, but the sound was more playful than exasperated. "Your lamps were supposed to arrive. Check the porch."

She heard shuffling on Dakota's end of the line. "Oh, yeah. There's a package. Where do these go again?"

"The ivory base with the green shade is for the living room. On the end table nearest the bookshelf. The blue one is for the master."

Dakota tore the tape. "I really didn't need lamps, Sis."

"Yes, you did. It's my job to make sure you have the things you didn't know you needed. You're welcome."

"Thanks. Any other surprises I should know about?"

"Hmm. Not that I can think of, but I'll let you know."

"Of course you will," Dakota mumbled.

"How are things?" The question may have sounded casual, but Dakota would tell her if he was having a hard time.

Dakota sighed. "Fine. Just working mostly. I'm helping Mr. Hart build a gazebo in his backyard, so that keeps me busy after work."

Sissy perked up at the mention of Tyler's father. "How are Mr. and Mrs. Hart doing?"

"Pretty good. They're still not used to being empty nesters. They invite me over for dinner almost every day."

"How sweet." Sissy rubbed her feet on the porch mat before walking inside. "I'm really proud of you."

"For what?" Dakota spat.

"For hanging in there. I know you miss her, but you're gonna be okay without her." Her brother wasn't the mushy type, so she didn't expect any commentary. "Just lean on the Lord, and I'll be praying for you. We're in this together."

"Thanks. Hey, I gotta run."

Sissy stepped into the kitchen and found Christy furiously chewing a bagel. "Call me later. Bye."

Dakota didn't reciprocate the farewell before disconnecting the call. Rude.

"Hey, lady. What's the hurry?" Sissy asked while Christy finished chewing.

Christy held up a finger, requesting a minute as she chugged a glass of water. She wiped her mouth and said, "I have a date."

"Ooh. Sweet! Anyone I know?"

"Nah. He's in my Chem class."

Sissy grabbed a pen and notepad from the kitchen counter. "I need names and locations."

Christy rolled her eyes, but her amused smile negated her attempt to seem irritated. "His name is Jackson, and we're going to Rounders."

Sissy jotted down the information. "Sounds like fun. Please be home by 9:00 sharp."

Christy threw her arms around Sissy's neck. "Thanks for looking out for me."

Sissy hugged her roommate and gave an extra squeeze. "We have to stick together."

"Always. I don't know what I would do without you." Christy pulled away and reached for the remainder of the bagel. "What are your plans for tonight?"

"Tyler wants to hang out. I'll call him in a little bit to see what he wants to do."

Christy waggled her eyebrows. "What is this, like, date number four?"

Sissy shrugged and dropped her attention to the

paper as she folded it. "I don't know. Tyler is weird about classifying our dates as dates."

"Are they dates? Is he allergic to commitment?"

Sissy squinted one eye as she deliberated. "I don't think so. I think he's just too cautious for his own good."

"Or maybe you aren't cautious enough," Christy offered.

"That's a fair assessment, but I know Tyler. He isn't a bad guy."

Christy grabbed the empty paper plate from the counter and tossed it in the trash. "If your best endorsement is that he isn't a bad guy, he might need a new PR team."

"Well, he's a good guy. Not because it's the opposite of a bad guy. He's been really good to me so far. He's just worried about the whole Dakota thing." Sissy waved her hand dismissively.

"Are you worried about it? What do you think he'll say when he finds out?"

Sissy chewed the inside of her cheek as she considered. "I really don't know. It's not worth bringing up just yet. Things are still new with Tyler."

It was true that their relationship was just getting started, but it had progressed enough that she really hoped things worked out. Her expectations were so high they were up in the stratosphere, and there wasn't much she could do to keep them in check. She had every reason to like Tyler, and she didn't really care what her brother thought of it.

Christy patted Sissy's shoulder on her way out. "Don't worry about it yet. Have fun tonight, and don't do anything I wouldn't do."

Sissy saluted her friend and pulled her phone from her pocket to text Tyler.

Sissy: What are you doing?

She heard the front door close as Christy left. The clock on the microwave read 6:35. Tyler may have already eaten dinner.

Her phone dinged with a text.

Tyler: Nothing.

Always with the single-word responses. She'd never had trouble carrying the conversation, but Tyler didn't give her much to work with.

Sissy: Dinner?
Tyler: Yes.
Sissy: Movie?
Tyler: Yes.
Sissy: My house?
Tyler: Yes.

Maybe there was something to this short and sweet communication style.

Tyler: I'll bring dinner. What would you like?

The conversation had leveled up to multi-word sentences and the date hadn't even begun.

Sissy: Surprise me.

She stuck the phone in her pocket and darted to her bedroom. Her shirt had pickled beet juice dripping down the front, so that needed to be changed. Sissy cringed at the sight. Claire's new favorite food was disgusting and left both of them smelling like vinegar.

Sissy hastily spritzed a sweet pea fragrance on her new shirt and pulled her hair from the messy bun. Looking in the mirror, she considered slapping on some makeup, but it seemed ridiculous to put on a full face of war paint just to take it off for bed in a few hours. Instead, she pinched the mounds of her cheeks and bit her lips. The old-fashioned tricks would work tonight.

It was Tyler's first time coming over, and though her place wasn't a mess, she spent what little extra time she had picking up and straightening things. By the time the doorbell chimed, she was singing "A Spoonful of Sugar" as she danced to the door.

When she opened the door, she fought to control her smile.

Tyler held two boxes—pizza on one side and donuts on the other. "Surprise."

"Wow. I did ask for a surprise. I thought you were bringing dinner, but I didn't expect dessert too. What made you bring donuts?"

He shrugged and nervously dropped his gaze. "I don't know. You seem like the kind of person who would like donuts."

"That's some good perception you got there, doc." She reached for the donut box and gasped when she opened the lid. It was a variety dozen in beautiful colors ranging from glazed blueberry to pink with sprinkles.

"I love..." She stopped, acutely aware of how close she'd been to word vomiting a playful profession of love that Tyler definitely would have taken seriously. He'd be running for the hills in a hot minute if she threw the L word at him this early. "I love sprinkles!"

Tyler's mouth tugged into a smile and his eyes softened. "I had a hunch."

Impulsively, she pushed up onto her toes to kiss his cheek. The slight stubble raked against her lips, leaving them tingling after she pulled away.

Before he had time to overanalyze anything, she grabbed his free hand and pulled him inside. "Come on. This food smells delicious."

Tyler might have hung back and slowly made his way into her home if she hadn't dragged him in. Hopefully, he'd have time to check out the scenery if he came over more.

"Welcome to my kitchen," Sissy dramatically announced. "This is where the magic happens." She winked at Tyler who was looking anywhere except at her. "Studying. I study here," she clarified.

Tyler nodded and placed the pizza box on the small kitchen island. "I hope you like pepperoni."

She placed a hand on his shoulder. "I do. Stop worrying. Thank you for being so determined to surprise me." Her hand trailed down his arm, and he tensed beneath her touch.

Tyler cleared his throat and looked around the kitchen.

"I'll get us some plates and drinks. What would you like?" she asked.

"Water, please."

She opened the fridge and grabbed a bottle for Tyler and the pitcher of sweet tea for herself. "Too many calories in the pizza?" she jested.

"Something like that," he murmured.

Sissy handed him a paper plate and watched as he lifted a slice onto his plate. "You don't like pizza, do you?"

Tyler turned to her with wide eyes. "Why do you think that?"

"Because you're handling it like it's toxic slime."

"It's not... I mean, it's not my favorite. I just..."

"You just got pizza because you thought I'd like it."

He tucked his chin and huffed. "Something like that."

Sissy laughed. "Tyler! That's crazy. You know that's crazy, right? I don't condone this self-sacrificing behavior."

"It's just dinner. I'll eat pizza."

"No. If you haven't had dinner, I'm cooking something good for you." She looked around the kitchen as she thought about her options. "Spaghetti?" she asked.

"Really, I can just eat the pizza."

"How about this time you eat the pizza, but next time I make something you'll like?" It didn't sit well with her that he wouldn't enjoy the meal.

He quirked one eyebrow. "You think there will be a next time?"

Sissy shoved his shoulder. "Yes, there will be. I don't think you have much choice now. You're stuck with me."

Tyler leaned back against the counter and crossed his arms over his chest. "I am?"

Did he know his defined muscles were distracting when he stood that way? Instead of overanalyzing it, she gripped both of his biceps and gave them a playful squeeze. Yep, hard as a rock.

While she was admiring his sculpted physique, Tyler's breath hitched. When she looked up at him, his gaze locked on hers.

She smiled when his attention dipped to her lips. "Yeah. Stuck like glue."

His breathing resumed, deep and heavy as his gaze flashed back to her eyes. "I'm okay with that."

Sissy tilted her head, pleased with his acceptance. "Okay enough to kiss in the kitchen?"

She waited a second and a half while he contemplated. Then she barely registered the moment when he made up his mind. He grabbed her arms and sealed his mouth with hers in an instant.

She inhaled the spice of his cologne and her skin tingled in a dizzying rush. If he hadn't been holding her arms, she might have melted like an ice cream cone in the hot Georgia summer. Speaking of hot, it seemed as if the temperature increased by twenty degrees.

Just as quickly as the kiss had consumed her, he pulled away.

His eyes remained closed, and his nostrils flared as

he inhaled. "I *do* want to kiss you in the kitchen. I just don't want that to be the only thing we do tonight." His eyes opened, and his gaze locked on hers. "That's not why I'm here."

A bubbly churning filled her middle as she looked up at him. He was special in the way she'd always hoped to find. "I know. You're here for rom coms and donuts." She grabbed one from the open box and took a big bite.

He shook his head. "That's not why I'm here either."

Oh, that deep, serious voice had her toes curling. Who knew Tyler's smolder had a max setting? She liked it a lot more than she wanted to admit.

Then his swoony, serious expression faded and was replaced by a knowing smirk. "Plus, I never agreed to a rom com."

Sissy gasped. "What? I was really looking forward to watching *Notting Hill*."

Tyler's eyes widened.

"Well, maybe not that one." She recalled the plot after she'd suggested it and realized the opposites attract story might hit too close to home.

"What about *My Best Friend's Wedding*?" she suggested.

Tyler's tense muscles relaxed. "We can watch whatever you want." He leaned in until his lips grazed her ear. His warm breath sent a chill down her spine. "I'm not here for the movie either."

He straightened, but Sissy was paralyzed, stunned

by Tyler's meaningful words. She often joked with him about his short responses, but he could pack a punch into a single sentence.

"Um." Sissy's attention darted around the room as she attempted to regain her bearings. "What were we doing? Oh! Food." She spoke quickly to cover her nervousness. "Yes, we should eat. But you don't like pizza. But we decided you'd eat it anyway. Well, I guess that's it. We're eating pizza. Then donuts. Then maybe some more kissing. I mean pizza!"

Tyler rested his hands on her shoulders. "Calm down. We're just eating."

"Right. Just eating," she repeated.

He smiled, and she instinctively smiled back as her nervousness evaporated. She'd had her share of dating disasters, but she knew Tyler wasn't going to leave her at the restaurant holding the bill or fill her in on what he "expected" after the meal. No, Tyler was a good one. She was beginning to believe he was the best one.

They ate standing at the kitchen island, and her temporary nervousness evaporated, allowing her to carry the conversation with stories and reenactments of her day with the Wilson kids. After they'd each had two slices of pizza, Sissy grabbed another donut and watched Tyler flash her a smirk as she licked her fingers.

"You know, hands are some of the filthiest parts of your body."

Sissy popped her thumb out of her mouth and kept her gaze locked on Tyler as she made a show of washing her hands then wiggling her fingers. "They're clean."

Tyler tucked his chin and shook his head. She wasn't sure if he'd ever get used to hanging out with her and her dirty hands, but when he didn't protest too much, it gave her hope.

She crept toward him, showing her clean hands. "Ready for a movie?"

Tyler nodded, seeming only marginally more comfortable. She grabbed his hand and skipped to the living room, dragging him behind her.

The small community room in the old house had a TV mounted above the fireplace, but Sissy and Christy had agreed when they moved in that the fireplace wouldn't be used. They had a good laugh about the lack of fireplace use in Hotlanta. The jagged brick walls weren't ideal for decorating, but Sissy had found ways around it. A string of bulb lights hung around the ceiling perimeter, and tall, ivory vases sprouting greenery sat at intervals around the room.

"We don't have a streaming service, but we have old-fashioned DVDs! Lucky for you, Christy has a great collection." Sissy gestured to the built-in bookshelf beside the hearth that was packed with DVD cases.

Tyler's gaze swiped over the options and quickly moved to Sissy. "You choose."

She rolled her eyes. "I'm never going to get to know you if you don't make decisions. Pizza, rom coms, dirty hands, spontaneous swimming sessions, what else is on the do-not-like list?"

"Nothing."

Sissy narrowed her eyes at him. "That's not true. I doubt you like salsa dancing and karaoke."

Tyler's eyes widened. "You'd be correct."

She pointed at the couch. "Sit. I'll pick." She dragged a finger over the various titles before grabbing one of her favorites. She hid the case behind her as she moved to the DVD player and stuck it in.

Tyler watched her with a curious expression as she grabbed the remote and jumped onto the couch beside him.

"You ready?" She pressed the button to skip to the DVD menu.

"*Jurassic Park*?" Tyler questioned.

Sissy clasped her hands at her chest. "Yes. I love it."

Tyler's brows rose. "That isn't the first time you've surprised me."

"And it won't be the last," she reminded him.

"You know this is—"

"Shh," she interrupted as she placed a finger on his lips. "I know you're an intelligent man, and *Jurassic Park* isn't real. Okay? This isn't the time to pick it apart with your sexy science brain."

Tyler's eyes widened, and he froze for a second before slowly nodding his acceptance. When she dropped her finger, his gaze shifted to her lips. That look made her stomach fall every time. Did he want to kiss her as badly as she wanted to be kissed?

"I'm glad you came over," she whispered, hoping to settle the nervousness rolling in her middle.

He shyly smiled and draped his arm across the back of the couch. She scooted closer, taking his silence as an affirmation that he was just as glad to be here.

The familiar score played, and the images moved over the screen, but Sissy wasn't interested in the movie. Tyler Hart was here, and somehow, the reality of spending time with him beat all of her childish hopes that he'd one day notice her.

Her favorite movie couldn't hold her attention with Dr. Smolder sitting beside her.

When Ian Malcolm began to explain the duty of scientists to tread carefully into research that was unchecked, Sissy slowly walked two fingers over her legs toward Tyler's hand resting on his thigh. She didn't have to wait for Tyler to get the hint. He opened his hand, allowing her to slide hers against his, locking their fingers together.

"Is this acceptable, Dr. Hart?" she asked playfully.

"As long as it's okay with you. I don't want you to feel pressured," he said with a serious stare.

When she realized he wasn't kidding, she giggled. "I am so far from pressured. We're on middle-school level right now."

"Not really," Tyler countered. "That kiss in the kitchen was hot."

She froze at the directness of his remark. Oh, Dr. Hart knew how to change the mood. Sissy suddenly found herself replaying the kiss and Tyler's firm, yet gentle admiration earlier.

"You're blushing," he said as he brushed his fingertips along her cheek. He followed the trail of his fingers for a moment before sliding his thumb along her jaw down to her chin.

With a gentle grip, he held her still as his lips brushed across hers. Control and adoration warred in his movements, comforting and sure.

When he pulled away, she inhaled deeply. "Are we dating? Like, are we together?" The question had been hanging out in the back of her mind, popping up each time her confidence slipped a fraction, and she wouldn't feel satisfied until Tyler spoke the word.

He hesitated, and she felt a blanket of doubt being pulled over her.

"Don't think about it. Just say one word."

"Yes," Tyler said, quick and certain.

She felt the muscles in her body relax from her head to her toes.

Tyler's gaze swept over every inch of her face. "This is all new to me."

"It's new to me too," she admitted.

He huffed, and the conflicted expression on his face had her confidence backing up.

"You were always my friend's sister, but things are different now. *You're* different now. We're both different. We're older. I admire you." He swallowed hard. "I'm still getting to know this new you—the fiery, passionate woman I can't get out of my head."

Her heart was working overtime, banging against the walls of her chest as if begging to escape.

And it had. Her heart didn't solely belong to her anymore. Tyler held a part that no one else had ever touched.

"You've changed," he whispered. "And you've changed me."

Doubt didn't exist here anymore. It was just her and Tyler now, and she hadn't been this excited about anything in years.

She rested her head on his shoulder, and they watched the rest of the movie without speaking a single word.

CHAPTER 12
Tyler

Tyler listened as he locked his office door on Thursday evening. His office was located in the back corner of the building, and he had two hallway options that would lead him to the exit. Choosing the path of least resistance had been a long-running game.

The high-pitched voice of Becky came from the hallway to his right. "I'll call you later, Jess!"

He might be able to avoid Becky if he walked slowly, but Jess was another nurse who might stop him to ask if he'd logged his notes in the patient records today. He had, but he still didn't like the interaction. It always ended with an eye roll and her grumbled whispers before he made it out of earshot.

The hallway to the left was quiet. He'd have to pass triage and a few offices, but they were probably empty this time of day.

He made it around the corner and had the exit in

sight when Lisa stepped out of Dr. Wilson's office. With the door at her back, she narrowed her eyes and sneered.

She shouldn't have anything to gripe at him about. He'd been a model of kindness for weeks, but she still didn't look happy.

Deciding to beat her to the punch, he nodded and said, "Have a good evening."

Her glare held as she turned and walked away from him. It was good to know that some things never changed. She was still ignoring him.

That went well. It was a step up from crossed arms and barbed words. He'd take what he could get.

Before Dr. Wilson's intervention and the introduction of Sissy into his life, he wouldn't have cared one way or the other what Lisa thought about him. It was just another indication of the shift in his life lately. Things were trending up.

His phone vibrated in his pocket as he reached his truck in the empty parking lot. Sissy didn't cut him any slack, and he liked that about her.

"Hello."

"Hey, handsome. How was work?"

Her upbeat tone contrasted to the monotony of his day and the gray walls of the clinic.

"Fine. Yours?"

"Fabulous! I aced another project, and I won a free cookie at Lucy Lou's Bakery!"

Tyler started the truck and switched the call to speaker. "That's great."

"So, I think we should celebrate. Let's have dinner tonight."

Tyler grinned as he shifted into reverse. "You're assuming I don't have plans, sweetheart."

Sissy gasped. "Do you have another date? Who is she?"

Her feigned outrage only widened his smile. "There's no one else. At least not another woman."

Sissy humphed.

"I have a men's prayer group meeting at 7:00 tonight."

"Will this *men's prayer group* be supervised? Should I see if Ms. Miller is available to chaperone?"

Tyler's skin crawled at the mention of Ms. Miller, the queen of the busybodies in Carson where he and Sissy grew up. "Please don't. There are enough women out for my head right now."

Sissy laughed, clearly entertained by her purposefully awful suggestion. "Oh, really? There are others?"

Tyler checked both ways twice before pulling out onto the main road. "Get in line. Did Dr. Wilson tell you that I've been on probation for bad behavior?"

Sissy cackled. That was the only word he could use to describe the uninhibited laughter.

"You think this is funny?" he asked. "My job is at stake."

"Oh, please. I'm sure it's not that serious, Dr. Drama pants."

"What does this have to do with my pants?"

"Nothing. Your pants are cute, unlike your attitude sometimes. I'm sure Dr. Wilson had good intentions when she put you in time out."

He knew she did, but he looked up to his mentor, and it didn't sit well with him that she was disappointed in his behavior. It brought back memories of fourth grade and the teacher who made him sit in the hallway during recess and write his spelling words and definitions over and over. Now he wondered if his social issues had been hindered during his year in the hallway or if he was always destined to be a jerk.

"I know. I'm making progress. I may need to send a muffin basket to the nurses though. I haven't won them over yet."

"Well, you won't do it with muffins. Try cookies. You can thank me later."

That was another reason why he needed Sissy. She continuously saved him. "Noted."

"Okay, so if you have your men's prayer meeting tonight, can I see you tomorrow?"

"The crawfish boil is tomorrow night. Did you forget?" It wasn't like Sissy to forget about an event. She lived for the get-togethers.

Sissy groaned. "I did forget, only because I wanted to. I hate crawfish."

Tyler slammed on the brakes a little too hard at the traffic light. "What? I thought you loved everything."

"I do. I love them as animals, but I dislike them as food. Even the smell makes me gag."

There were still so many things to learn about Sissy. Would they ever get to the point when they would know everything about each other? It seemed like a more daunting task than usual, given Sissy's impulsive nature. If she didn't like something, it was probably because she hadn't tried it yet.

"Does that mean you're not going?" Tyler asked.

"Umm. Probably. I hate to miss it, but..." She trailed off as if conflicted.

"Don't feel pressured to go if you don't want to. I volunteered to help clean up after, since I knew I'd be late getting there after work. Now I wish I hadn't."

"No, no," Sissy said. "You should go and have fun."

Tyler often had a hard time having fun, but it seemed easier these days with Sissy around. "I don't know about the fun part."

"We could have told everyone about us! Oh, but I wouldn't want to steal Brian's birthday thunder."

Tyler hadn't realized what attending the party together actually meant. Most of their friends ran in the same circles, and they hadn't revealed their relationship to anyone yet—mostly because he was a chicken and didn't want to face Dakota.

"Are you ready to tell them?" he asked. He didn't want to hurt her feelings if she misinterpreted his hesitation, but he wasn't anywhere near ready to reveal their relationship.

"Why not? It's not like it's going away. We can't keep it a secret forever."

She had a point. Why were they hiding it?

Oh yeah, Dakota. Tyler's best friend who wouldn't

take too kindly to being blindsided with "I've been dating your little sister for a month and didn't tell you."

Tyler tried to focus on the road ahead, but a million thoughts were whirling in his head. "How should we tell Dakota?"

"I don't know. Won't you see him tomorrow night?"

"Yeah. I could tell him then." He wasn't a coward, but he wasn't eager to lay this bomb on his friend.

"Or I could send him a text," Sissy offered.

"No, no." If he didn't get ahead of her quickly, she'd have the text fired off before they got off the phone call.

"Okay, suit yourself. Good luck with that. Should I arrange for a cookie basket for him too?"

Tyler sighed as he pulled into his driveway. He had ten minutes to change and get on the road to the church. "It wouldn't hurt."

* * *

Tyler scanned the parking lot as he pulled around to the side lot at the church he attended in an Atlanta suburb near his house. The men's prayer group met in the fellowship hall on the first Thursday night of every month, and he'd invited Dakota this time. There may have been bribery involved, but Tyler wasn't above using donuts to sweeten the deal.

He recognized the handful of vehicles in the

parking lot, but none were Dakota's faded Bronco. Brother Jerry was leading the message tonight, and Tyler wanted his friend here for this one. He knew Dakota went to church regularly, but maybe a male-centered group would let him know he wasn't alone in this fight.

Tyler checked his phone for a missed call or a message from Dakota. Nothing. And there were only five minutes to spare.

Stopping just outside the side door that led straight into the fellowship hall, Tyler made the call. He didn't want to be the nagging friend, but isn't that what Dakota had asked of him? Accountability?

The ringing ended, and a robotic voice said, "Your call has been forwarded to an automated voice messaging system."

Tyler huffed and looked up the road. Another truck was pulling in, but it wasn't Dakota.

It wasn't a big deal, but it was. Tyler had talked to Dakota just yesterday, and they'd planned to night fish after the meeting. Even if Dakota wasn't gung-ho about men's prayer group, he wouldn't miss night fishing.

Tyler was still chewing the inside of his cheek when Danny walked up and greeted him with a smile he couldn't return.

"Hey, man. How's it goin'?"

Tyler rolled his phone over in his hand. "Been better. A friend was supposed to meet me here, and I'm not sure he's coming."

Danny's eyes squinted. "I know that feeling. I have a hard time letting the people I care about make the decision on their own."

"He's a believer, but he's struggling with something big right now. He needs this." Tyler huffed and scanned the parking lot again. "I wish he could understand how important this is."

Danny patted Tyler's shoulder. "Come on inside. We'll all pray for him tonight."

Tyler nodded, knowing that was the reason they gathered—to pray for those in need, their church, and the community. "Yeah, okay." He followed Danny inside with a heavy feeling in his gut. Dakota should be here. It wasn't like him not to show up for something they'd planned.

It took Tyler longer than usual to assemble his hamburger. He was too busy watching the door. His head popped up every time the metal door clanged. Even after he'd taken his seat, he couldn't focus on the conversations around him.

After Brother Jerry blessed the food, Tyler slipped out to the parking lot. The muggy summer heat greeted him, only furthering his irritation. His breathing grew deeper as the call rang in his ear.

"Your call has been—"

Tyler ended the call with a finger tap that he wished was a thump on Dakota's thick skull. Tyler rubbed his brow and took a deep breath before calling Brian.

"Hey, doc," Brian answered.

"Have you heard from Dakota this evening?" Tyler asked.

"Can't say I have. You lookin' for him?"

"Yes. He was supposed to meet me ten minutes ago."

The hesitation on the other end of the call meant Brian knew at least a little about Dakota's recent spiral.

"I'll run by his place," Brian said before ending the call.

Great, now there wasn't anything to do except go back inside, stomach the hamburger he didn't want, and try not to think about Sissy's missing brother that Tyler somehow felt responsible for locating.

The cold air welcomed him back inside the fellowship hall. Brother Jerry hadn't taken his place at the small podium, so Tyler was able to sneak back to his seat without being noticed.

"Hey, man," Keith said as Tyler took his seat.

Well, almost unnoticed.

"Hey, how's the office?" Keith was a local veterinarian, and he never turned down the chance to talk about work.

"Oh, it's great. Just bumpin' along."

Come on, Keith. I need a puppy story tonight. Keep talking. Anything to keep the conversation pointed away from Tyler would work.

"You okay?" Henderson asked. "You're glistening a little more than usual." Henderson was a local farmer who liked to poke fun at the men with desk jobs. It was all in good fun, but Tyler didn't appreciate the attention tonight.

"Yeah, it's hot outside."

Okay, something was definitely wrong. He was making obvious statements that would put Brian's ineptness to shame.

Tyler's phone buzzed in his pocket, and he jumped up. "I need to take this."

"Must be on call," Keith said at the table.

Once again, Tyler found himself subject to the scorching heat at sundown, and he answered the call with an irritated tone. "Did you find him?"

"I did. He's... fine," Brian said, but his tone wasn't assuring.

"How fine? Where is he?" Tyler wasn't a fan of beating around the bush, and Brian was the worst at delivering concise information.

"He's at his house."

"How did you get there so quickly?" Tyler asked.

"I was at Barbara's. She had something for Mom and asked me to come by and pick it up."

Tyler's heart beat harder. "How is Dakota?"

"For lack of a better word, he's trashed."

Tyler gripped the phone and fought the urge to chuck it at the brick wall. "You've got to be kidding me."

"Wish I was, but he's pretty worthless this evening. He won't be meeting you anywhere."

Tyler huffed in exasperation. Things with Dakota

were getting worse instead of better. "Does Barbara know about this?"

"Not that I know of," Brian said.

"How often is he like this?" Tyler asked. Brian didn't sound too surprised to find Dakota in his incapacitated state, so he had to know at least a little about what was going on.

"It comes and goes. Sometimes five days in a row, but sometimes it's just three days a week."

Tyler bit back a curse. Dakota was flat out drunk three to five days a week, and he didn't think he needed help. He was about to get a rude wakeup call.

"Thanks for finding him. I wouldn't call if—"

"I know," Brian interrupted. "We're all concerned. I'm glad you called. Someone needed to check on him tonight."

Dakota had a handful of great friends willing to help him, but how much babysitting could they really do? If things got any worse, they'd be giving him an in-person wake-up call each morning to make sure he made it to work.

The buck was about to stop here. Dakota's dad had died years ago, so the best kick in his pants he was going to get was from Tyler.

CHAPTER 13
Sissy

"Hey, ladies!" Sissy called out as she walked into the church kitchen.

"Well, there she is!" Mrs. Nesmith bellowed. "I thought you'd for sure have plans on a Friday night."

Sissy gestured to her overalls. "I do. I'm here to work." She liked having a socially packed schedule, but she also didn't mind having a Friday night off to help out with the Loaves and Fishes ministry. Their small church packed dozens of meals for kids in low-income families to take home over the weekend.

She hadn't seen Tyler in a few days, and she needed a distraction. He wasn't ignoring her, thankfully. Their schedules just hadn't worked out this week. Tonight, she needed to get her mind off of the creepy, crawly crawfish Tyler would be eating with their friends. She shivered just thinking about it.

Mrs. Nesmith wrapped an arm around Sissy's

shoulder and led her into the kitchen. "We can put you to work, sweetheart, but you're the entertainment tonight."

Sissy smiled and reached to hug another familiar face. "You can count on me." Most of the church ladies were a good quarter of a century older than her, and they always got a kick out of her college and babysitting shenanigans.

"Did I hear you have a boyfriend?" Mrs. Eads asked.

"I sure do!" Sissy put her hands on her hips, looking and feeling proud to receive an opportunity to brag about her handsome catch. "He's a *doctor*."

"What? Which one?" Miss Caldwell asked, as if she were on a first-name basis with every doctor in town.

"Tyler Hart. He's finishing up his residency at the Boshell Clinic."

"Oh, at Dr. Wilson's place? Her daughter takes dance lessons with my Janie Mae," Mrs. Nesmith said, ever eager to mention her granddaughter.

Sissy couldn't blame her. Janie Mae was a sweetheart. "You know I babysit Claire," Sissy reminded her.

"I did know that. It just slipped my mind. Dr. Wilson is a good one. I bet your man loves working with her."

"I think he does," Sissy said with a grin. "She's the one who introduced us."

Mrs. Eads slapped a hand on the counter next to a dozen cans of chicken noodle soup. "Well, it's a small world."

"It sure is," Sissy agreed.

"Has he been married before? Have any kids?" Mrs. Eads asked.

"What? No!" Sissy bellowed. "He doesn't have a secret family or a bloody axe in his closet either."

"Are you sure?" Miss Caldwell asked. "You never know with people these days."

Sissy huffed. Tyler was as close to Honest Abe as he could get. Now that he felt comfortable with her, she felt assured that nothing was off-limits. Honesty and loyalty meant a lot to her, and they were a big reason why she was so caught up in Tyler Hart.

"This isn't *To Catch a Killer*. He's just a normal guy."

"Okay, now I know you're lying. You would never be interested in anyone who is just a normal guy," Miss Caldwell said. "You're too spirited for that."

"Oh, speaking of extra. I need to get the rest of the box meals out of my car," Mrs. Eads announced as she grabbed her car keys.

"You need help?" Sissy asked.

"I can always use a hand."

Sissy followed Mrs. Eads out to her vehicle. It was an older model Buick, but the paint job was still shiny, and there wasn't a speck of dirt on it.

They loaded their arms with grocery bags filled with complete box meals and headed back into the church.

When they entered the kitchen, the hushed tones

and whispers quietened. They set the bags on the counter, and one of the ladies cleared her throat.

"Hun," Miss Caldwell said in a placating tone. "We're sorry. We shouldn't have assumed there was some big dark secret to learn about your boyfriend. We all know that if you're hangin' onto him, then he's a good one."

Sissy scrunched her mouth to the side, touched by the ladies' assurances and apology. "Come here, you old goat." Sissy pulled her into a hug and loudly whispered in Miss Caldwell's ear, "You need a new soap opera."

The ladies laughed in unison. The cheerful sound drove out any weight that may have lingered from the grilling she'd endured.

Miss Caldwell looked up at Sissy with a sweet smile. "We love you, and we're happy for you." Then, she raised her voice. "I don't know about you ladies, but I feel like prayin'."

A chorus of "Amen" rang out in the kitchen, and Sissy bowed her head along with the others.

Miss Caldwell took a deep breath before beginning. "Lord, we weren't Christ-like to our sister this evening. We weren't listening with our hearts, and we spoke while our minds were far from You. Help us to encourage our sister, and we pray You will guide her new relationship. In Jesus' name we pray. Amen."

Sissy squeezed Miss Caldwell's hand as the prayer ended. "I sure appreciate that. I've been prayin' for a good man for a long time, and I think I've finally found him."

"Is he treatin' you right?" Mrs. Eads asked.

"Of course," Sissy assured. "I wouldn't be gushin' about him to y'all if he wasn't."

"Oh, we know," Mrs. Eads said. "We just look out for you like our own. You deserve a good man."

"It's all in the Lord's timing." Sissy shrugged. "Actually, Tyler and I grew up together. So, we've known each other for years, but I guess that wasn't our time, you know?"

A chorus of awws filled the room.

"We have to start packing meals!" Mrs. Eads proclaimed. "We're never going to get out of here if we keep hemin' and hawin' over Sissy's young love life."

"Amen," Mrs. Nesmith shouted. "Norma, will you lead the singin'?"

Sissy had missed these women. She'd missed the fellowship with her church friends, the good ministry they were doing, and the hymns they sang as they packed meals for the kids. The evening passed in melody and worship, but her heart was often reminded of Tyler. She was happy to be with her friends, but she missed him. How had he carved out such a gigantic and meaningful part of her heart in such a short time?

And why was *this* their time? Telling the other ladies about her history with Tyler made her wonder why their paths had never crossed to bring them together until now.

When the meals were packed and blessed with

prayer, Sissy said good night to everyone with an enthusiastic hug. These ladies were her soul sisters, and she loved them more than pizza and sweet tea.

"We love you," Mrs. Eads said as they hugged each other and waved good-bye in the parking lot.

"Love you too." Sissy slid into her car and heard her ringtone for Lindsey. She answered quickly so she could move the call to speakerphone before she pulled out of the parking lot. "Hey, girl!"

"Hey. What are you up to?" Lindsey asked.

"Just leaving the church. We packed meals tonight."

"Fun," Lindsey said. A long yawn followed.

"What about you?" Sissy asked as she backed out. Her headlights illuminated the parking lot.

"Just hanging out at the apartment. It's been a long week." Lindsey's voice was weak and sounded sad.

"You okay, friend? Do I need to come visit?" Sissy had flown to see her best friend in New York City before, and she'd do it again if needed.

"You're so sweet to offer. I really wish *I* could come to *you*. It's so busy here, and I'm always trying to keep my head above water."

"I thought you wanted the busy life," Sissy said.

"I did. I do. Sometimes. I'm just never going to be able to save up enough money to come visit you. I miss you." Lindsey's voice cracked, and she began to cry. "I miss home."

"Oh, sweetie. It's okay. Let's video chat when I get home. You need to see a friendly face."

"Thank you," Lindsey cried shakily. "I love you."

"Love you too, Lindz. I'll call you right back."

Sissy sped home knowing Christy was on a date and Tyler was at Brian's birthday party. There would be nothing keeping her from giving her faraway friend a good pick-me-up.

Storming inside, Sissy threw her purse and keys onto the entry table and jogged to her room. Well, jogging was a little ambitious. She hustled, which required less constructed effort. Within minutes, she had her makeup off and her favorite PJs on—the ones covered in llamas wearing sunglasses that read, "Save the drama for your llama." She'd almost worn out the elastic in the waist, but she'd be sewing these babies back together when they decided to give out.

She spent a good three minutes searching for her laptop before finding it tucked beneath a couch pillow. She'd forgotten about falling asleep in the living room after ordering a gray-and-blue geometric shower curtain for one of Dakota's bathrooms. Slowly but surely, she was piecing his house together. With his construction and her design, the place was going to be amazing when it was completed.

She powered up the laptop and ran to the kitchen for a drink. Her original mission had been for water, but the chocolate milk she'd bought earlier this week was staring her in the face, begging to be consumed. She grabbed it without a second thought and headed back to the living room. She plopped onto the couch and tapped the video chat app, ready for an evening of girl talk.

Lindsey answered quickly. "Hey, lady." She looked paler than she used to, and she'd recently dyed her hair, covering up the blonde she'd worn for years in favor of her natural chocolate brown.

"Have I told you how much I love your hair?" Sissy beamed.

"Only every time we see each other." Lindsey rolled her eyes. "I'm glad you like it because I can't afford to color it anymore."

Lindsey's voice trailed off, and Sissy could sense the unease of her words. She hated that her friend was going through a hard time. She wanted to wrap her arms around her and hug the sadness away, but thousands of miles separated them.

She wished Lindsey had stayed in Carson. She also wished Lindsey hadn't broken things off with Dakota when she left. There was a lot of distance, but Dakota would have done anything to make things work—including building her a custom home in the place she'd always loved. Well, the place she'd loved until the New York City lights blinded her.

Sissy wanted Lindsey to chase her dreams. She believed in her friend. She'd also loved her enough not to argue with her when she thought running the entertainment rat race would be her dream come true.

"What's your poison tonight?" Sissy asked, holding up her own glass of thick and creamy chocolate milk.

Lindsey sighed deep enough that her shoulders rose and fell before pointing to a nearby glass of water.

Sissy scrunched her nose. "Eww. That's not good for you. Try again."

"I can't," Lindsey whispered.

"You know a milkshake would put a smile on your face. Doctor's orders."

"I have an audition tomorrow."

"Sorry, boo," Sissy consoled.

Lindsey tucked her feet beneath her and got more comfortable on her plain-Jane apartment couch. "Speaking of doctors, how are things with Tyler?"

"Somewhere between changing his phone number and a December wedding."

Lindsey laughed. It made Sissy's heart happy to hear the sound.

"I hope you didn't run him off. Why aren't you with him on a Friday night?"

Sissy didn't think it would help Lindsey at all to tell her Tyler was hanging out with all of their old friends, including Dakota, so she simplified the answer. "He's at some get-together. Plus, I needed to help out at church, so it worked out."

Lindsey rested her cheek against the back of the couch. "I'm glad y'all finally got together."

"Ha!" Sissy quipped. "It's not like this was years in the making. I had to dig my heels in and stand in front of him to get him to hang around for our blind date."

Lindsey covered her face to hide her giggles. "You're a mess."

"A fabulous mess." Sissy flipped her hair, then started surfing through the cable channels. "Ohh, let's watch *Cake Boss*." Thankfully, Lindsey's roommate splurged for cable.

Lindsey picked up the remote. "Let me find it."

A no-drama show usually helped Lindsey's mood if she was feeling down, and they both loved the outrageous cake designs.

"Thanks, Sis," Lindsey whispered.

Sissy winked at her friend. "Always."

She'd do whatever she could to cheer up the people in her life. Their happiness was just as important as their physical health.

Maybe she and Tyler would make a good healing team. He could heal their bodies, and she could bring joy to their hearts.

CHAPTER 14
Tyler

The sky was still bright when Tyler pulled into the long drive at his friend Jake's house. It was a modest place that sat in the middle of an old nine-hole golf course. The previous owners had lived there, but they'd converted the garage into a pro-shop and run the par 3 for decades.

Tyler and his friends had played this course since they were kids. It was cheap and good for practice or a day of goofing off. He was glad Jake had snagged the place. None of them wanted someone else to move in and let the course go.

There were already a dozen trucks parked in front of the house. Folding tables were lined up in the side yard, and a few fryers were being manned by people he recognized. A group of women sat cross-legged on the small front porch talking.

Tyler parked his truck to the side of the others. He'd be here later helping clean up, and he didn't want to block anyone in. He'd just grabbed his baseball cap from the passenger seat when he spotted his friend, Marcus. He didn't look happy, but he never did. His dark eyes and shaggy hair didn't give off welcoming vibes.

Tyler stepped out. "Hey, man."

"You talked to Dakota?" Marcus asked. His eyes were hidden in the shadow of his cap.

Concern grew in Tyler's chest. He wasn't in the mood to chase down his friend again. "Not today, but he said he'd be here."

Marcus nodded toward Tyler's truck. "Let's go."

Tyler huffed but kept his grumblings to himself. Marcus was probably just as irritated, and it wouldn't do them any good to sit around and whine about it. The fun and games were over before they got started.

Tyler started the truck. "The barn?"

"Probably a good place to start. I texted Joe, and he said Dakota was at work today, but they got off early when the rain came through after lunch."

That meant Dakota could have been drinking for hours. Tyler would call this mission a success if they found their friend upright, but he didn't have much hope. Hanging out with friends helped keep Dakota's mind off losing Lindsey, and it said a lot that he wasn't here early.

The sun was setting as they drove toward the pond. The tension in the truck eased a fraction when the headlights illuminated Dakota's Bronco parked in front of the old barn. At the bank, Dakota sat with his knees pulled up and his head hanging between them. A rod and plastic tackle box lay discarded in the thick grass beside him.

Tyler shifted the truck to park and killed the engine. "Let's do this." It was as much of a pep talk as he had in him. They were both dreading the storm they were walking into. Dakota was more like a lightning storm—potentially dangerous and unpredictable.

Dakota didn't raise his head as Tyler and Marcus approached.

Marcus didn't waste time. He kicked Dakota in the side with the toe of his boot. "Get up."

"Back off." The rage in Dakota's words was thick and heavy, mixing with Marcus's irritation.

Tyler's own fury was mounting. Couldn't Dakota see that he was only hurting himself? Drinking didn't make him feel better. He looked much worse than the last time Tyler had seen him.

"Get up," Marcus growled. "I'm sick of this pity party. You got somewhere to be."

"I'm not going," Dakota spat.

Marcus huffed. "Because you can't tell your right foot from your left? Pull it together, man. We're tired of pickin' you up. You're worse than my brothers, and they're half your age."

"Whatever." Dakota threw a rock into the water, and it landed with a *thunk*, disrupting the peaceful sunset reflecting on the surface.

Tyler crossed his arms over his chest. "How long have you been here?"

Dakota shrugged.

Marcus picked up a bottle of whiskey that had fallen over in the grass. There was about an inch of the amber liquid left. "Is this your first or second liter?"

"It's the second," Tyler answered for him as he retrieved an empty bottle hidden in the tall grass nearby. "You've gotta be kidding me."

Marcus grabbed Dakota by the upper arm and jerked, and he was stumbling to his feet in a split second.

Tension coiled in Tyler's shoulders. Marcus's strength was fueled by anger, but Dakota was built thick like a tree trunk. It was hard to imagine Dakota getting thrown around like a rag doll, but Tyler was seeing it with his own eyes.

"Dude, lay off!" Dakota growled as he shoved out of Marcus's hold on him. "I said I'm not going." His breaths came in deep waves as his nostrils flared and his jaw tensed.

Dakota was slipping more and more, and it turned Tyler's stomach to watch it play out. Not only was his friend hurting himself, but Sissy would be crushed if she found out what her brother was hiding from her. She'd want to help, and she would know how to motivate him to stay on track. Sissy had a way with things like that, unlike Tyler who seemed to send patients running away in tears. Sissy could help them both if Dakota wasn't so worried about disappointing her or being a burden.

Tyler tilted his chin toward the truck. "Take him home in his truck. I'll pick you up."

Marcus nodded before jerking Dakota's arm again, leading him to the Bronco parked by the barn.

"Why can't you just leave me alone?" Dakota growled. "I was doin' just fine on my own."

He stumbled, but Marcus kept his firm hold, ignoring the grumbling. There was a reason he handled his siblings so well. He couldn't be swayed by whining and complaining, and his patience was greater than most of their friends'.

But tonight, he'd had enough. They'd both had enough.

Tyler's headlights followed the Bronco to Dakota's house. It was just over the hill, but they had to drive out to the main road to go back up the path leading to the house.

Tyler helped Marcus wrangle Dakota inside. He twisted and grumbled a few times, but his resistance was minimal. They tossed Dakota on the couch where he landed hard on the firm cushions.

With a finger pointed at Dakota's frowning face, Tyler seethed, "I'm sick of this. You need help, and it isn't us."

"I don't need help," Dakota protested, but it was half-hearted.

"Yeah, I don't want to hear it tonight. We'll talk about it tomorrow when you're sober and I bring your truck keys back."

Dakota narrowed his eyes and glared between his

two friends. "You're kidding. You're not taking my keys."

Dakota scrambled to stand, but Marcus laid a heavy hand on his friend's shoulder and shoved him back down.

"Yes, he is," Marcus confirmed. The two men glared at each other for a moment before Dakota relented and fell back against the couch.

Marcus stalked for the door, and Tyler gave Dakota one last look. His face and arms were covered in a sheen of sweat, his shorts were muddy, and the whites of his eyes had a bloody tint.

"I'll be back in the morning." Tyler didn't wait to hear his friend's protests or complaints as he followed Marcus outside.

They didn't speak as they climbed back into the truck. Their mission was reluctantly completed, but there was the sinking realization that they hadn't accomplished anything good this evening.

"He needs help," Tyler finally said, breaking the silence that filled the dark cab of the truck.

"It won't do him any good if he doesn't snap out of it and do something to help himself," Marcus said.

Words stuck in Tyler's throat as he thought about Sissy. He'd been asked to keep a secret from her, and now it felt like more of a lie.

He took a deep breath and decided to spit it out. "Sissy needs to know."

Marcus turned his attention toward Tyler. "Why?"

"She worries about him. She would know how to help him."

"It's none of her business," Marcus countered.

"It *is* her business. She already lost her dad, and she can't lose her brother too."

The silence settled over them again like a thick blanket, clogging in Tyler's chest.

Finally, Marcus spoke. "You're seeing her, aren't you?"

Tyler tightened his jaw and focused on the section of road lit by the headlights, but he didn't answer.

Marcus hung his head. "You've got to be kidding me," he seethed.

"It's not like I meant for this to happen," Tyler defended, louder than anything else they'd spoken tonight.

"Oh, so you just accidentally started dating Kota's little sister? He's gonna lose his mind."

"Why? It's not like I'm a bad guy!" What was so wrong with the idea of him and Sissy being in a relationship?

"You don't see anything wrong with this?" Marcus mocked. "Lindsey is Sissy's best friend. If Sissy ends up with his best friend and actually makes it work…"

"Lindsey leaving Dakota doesn't have anything to do with me. It's not my fault she wanted to move away." It wasn't his fault, but Tyler knew there was at least a hint of truth in Marcus's words, and the realization felt like a hot knife sliding into his chest.

"Don't tell him yet. At least, not until we get him back on his feet."

Frustration mounted in Tyler's middle. He didn't so much care if people knew about his relationship with Sissy. But he did care that they were just getting started and he was being asked to choose between his best friend and the woman he cared about. Sissy didn't deserve to be lied to, especially when it involved her brother.

"Someone needs to tell her," Tyler said. "He's getting worse. The longer we wait, the harder it'll be on everyone. She's already going to be upset that he's kept this from her."

Marcus rubbed his brow. "It's going to upset her, but I'm not sure what to do. I don't know that she could help him."

Sure, there was that argument, but Tyler still felt uncomfortable knowing what he knew about her brother and purposefully not saying anything to her about it.

"We'll figure it out," Marcus assured.

Right now, Tyler wasn't sure they would be able to get Dakota the help he needed on their own. Tyler had sent multiple Alcoholics Anonymous meeting notices to his friend, and the suggestions were falling on deaf ears.

"I'm gonna head back over there," Tyler said. "I don't feel right leaving him alone tonight."

Marcus slapped a hand on Tyler's shoulder.

"You're a better man than I am. Let me know if you need help."

"Thanks." The offer was appreciated, but he knew Marcus was the guardian of his siblings, and he couldn't always run out at a moment's notice.

Marcus got out, and Tyler turned his truck back the way he'd just come.

CHAPTER 15
Sissy

Sissy clutched her Bible to her chest as Mrs. Ericson explained how to make her famous chicken and dressing. Sissy had asked for the recipe weeks ago, and she'd assumed Mrs. Ericson would bring it to her on a piece of paper, probably meticulously written in slanted handwriting. Everyone over the age of sixty-five seemed to have learned to write in the exact same way.

Instead of receiving the recipe in written form, Mrs. Ericson had cornered Sissy after Sunday School to give her the play-by-play verbal recipe.

"You use a Springer Mountain Farms chicken. No other kind will do. Oh, and you have to pull the strings off the celery. It's no good if you don't. That takes me about an hour and a half. You can start on that the day before. And go ahead and make your cornbread in a cast iron skillet, of course."

She hadn't understood a word Mrs. Ericson had

said, mostly because Sissy's attention kept darting to the glass doors that revealed the parking lot just beyond. Tyler was on his way, and she'd been hanging around the entrance waiting for him when Mrs. Ericson caught her.

Finally, Sissy spotted Tyler's old, gray truck pulling into the lot. She listened as Mrs. Ericson detailed the amount of sage for the dressing using the cupped palm of her hand.

"Now, if you get too much, it's better to start scooping it out than to leave it. Too much sage and the whole thing isn't worth a hoot."

"I'll remember that. Thanks so much for going through that with me. I'd love it if you would call me next time you're planning to make it. Maybe I can come by and help while I learn. We can cut that half-a-day prep time down to a few hours if we work together."

Mrs. Ericson patted Sissy on the cheek and gave her a pitying look. "That's what's wrong with you kids. You always want to cut corners. It ain't any good if you don't put the time into it."

Sissy stretched her grin and slowly nodded. "You're right. We should all probably slow down and make the dressing the correct way."

She didn't have any objection to taking the whole day to make the chicken and dressing. She just wondered how Mrs. Ericson proposed she make the other Thanksgiving side dishes while she spent the majority of the day preparing one dish.

The door opened and Sissy's attention jerked to Tyler. His greeting smile said more than a thousand words, and she didn't so much care anymore that Mrs. Ericson had reprimanded her for a lack of patience.

Sissy understood because what she had with Tyler was worth the wait.

"Thank you again. I'll call you if I have any questions," Sissy said.

Mrs. Ericson was already moving on to the next person she intended to greet when Sissy turned to Tyler.

"Hey, handsome." She slid her hand down the front of his shirt and rose up onto her toes to plant a sweet kiss on his cheek. She rarely saw him so early in the day, and his normal stubble was missing. It took all her willpower to keep from going back for more of those smooth kisses.

"Beautiful," Tyler whispered.

Her chest grew warm when he talked pretty to her. Tyler could pack a lot of meaning into one word—something she was growing to appreciate.

"Come on," Sissy said as she grabbed his hand. "We better start toward our seats. I expect to be stopped at least a handful of times before we get there. Lots of ladies will be eager to meet you."

Tyler gently resisted. "What?"

"Well, I told them about you. I may have bragged about my hot doctor boyfriend a little bit."

"Sissy." The exasperation in his tone did nothing to stop her toes from curling when he said her name.

"Yes?"

"What did you tell them?" he asked.

"Only truths!" she promised.

Tyler sighed before taking his place beside her and wrapping his arm around her waist. She enjoyed standing at his side more than she'd like to admit.

Mrs. Eads caught sight of them first and almost knocked Jerry off his feet in her hasty trip across the church. "Well, this must be the Dr. Hart you've been tellin' us about." She gave Tyler a once-over from his head to his toes and back up again.

He extended a hand. "Tyler Hart. It's a pleasure to meet you."

"Betty Eads. The pleasure is mine, doctor."

Miss Greyson was next, and she stuck herself to Mrs. Eads's side as she offered her greeting. "Nancy Greyson. We've heard all about you from Sissy."

Tyler's blush was beginning to bloom on his face, and spots were starting to crop up on his neck. He'd be covered in the rosy tint before they could get safely to their seats.

Sissy laid a hand on his shoulder and smiled at her friends. They knew what they were doing. She'd told them about his aversion to compliments—something she didn't really understand herself. "Please excuse us. I need to show Tyler where we'll be sitting."

The ladies allowed them to move on with sweet good-byes and waves, but Tyler leaned over to whisper in her ear.

"We have assigned seating?"

"Of course not. Don't you know everybody sits in the same seats every week?" She pointed to the pew a few rows ahead of them where five ladies sat. Each of them wore the same permed white hair and chatted with other members of the congregation. "That's the widows' pew."

"The what?" Tyler asked with wide eyes.

Sissy waved her hand dismissively. "Oh, they're fine. Their husbands died a decade ago, and they bonded over their shared grief. They've been the best of friends ever since. They visit the shut-ins every Wednesday and take them lunch and donuts."

"That's nice," Tyler said as he sat beside Sissy. His attention scanned the church for a moment before returning to her. "Thanks for inviting me."

He squeezed her hand, and she rested her head on his shoulder.

"I'm glad you're here. I mean, I'm just glad we're here together. I'm still up for going to your church next week." They'd only briefly talked about their different churches, and both were willing to try out the other place.

The service was powerful as always. Sissy loved Brother Grant's messages, and today's reminder about doubts and truth were especially insightful. Thomas was a doubter, but he soon learned the truth.

"How many of you have turned your back on the truth? How many of you have doubted because you were scared of the truth? We're not so different from Thomas, you know. He'd been hearing the word of the

Lord for over three years, day in and day out, and he *still* wasn't sure. Let me tell you, the truth is here." Brother Grant tapped the front of the Bible sitting before him. "We're encouraged to seek out the truth in our lives and in our faith. You'll find it here."

Sissy snuck a glance at Tyler, but he seemed engrossed in Brother Grant's words. She smiled, knowing Tyler took the education of his faith so seriously. And she shouldn't have expected any less. He was an academic, after all. He read textbooks and research articles constantly, and he often explained them to her. She loved the way his eyes lit up while telling her about an extra fascinating breakthrough in medicine. She understood the things he talked about as much as she understood Greek, but she could listen to him talk about his passion for medicine day and night.

After church they went to a small diner in Tyler's neighborhood for lunch. He held her hand as they walked in, and he gestured for her to choose their table.

She tucked her skirt behind her legs and scooted into her side of the booth. "So, you come here often?"

Tyler didn't pick up his menu. "About three times a week. They have a good BLT."

Sissy was already scanning the selection. "Hmm. That sounds yummy, but so does the Alabama burger. Fried green tomatoes on a burger is genius."

A dark-haired woman with a motherly smile stepped up to their table. "Hey, y'all. I'm Donna, and I'll be taking care of you today. What can I get you to start with?"

"Hey, Donna. I'd like sweet tea, please," Sissy said.

Tyler sat with his hands clasped atop his menu and waited until Donna looked his way. "Water."

"Y'all ready to order?" Donna asked.

"Um, sure," Sissy said. "I'll have the Alabama burger with fries."

"And you, sir?"

"The BLT, please."

"Toasted bread as always?"

"Yes."

Donna took their menus and sauntered to the kitchen.

"So, you have a usual here?" Sissy quipped. "And Donna still calls you sir. She's a sweetheart to remember your order."

"I guess so. I never really took note of her name until now."

Sissy gaped for a moment. "How have you not made friends with that angel? She knows your order, but you don't know her name?"

Tyler shrugged. "I just never really thought it mattered."

Sissy laid her hand atop his on the table. "Honey, you've got a long way to go. Stick with me, and I'll get you squared away. You'll have so many friends you won't know what to do with yourself."

"I'm not really a friends kinda person," Tyler said.

"So, Brian isn't your friend? I mean, you drove an hour to spend the evening at his birthday party. You grew up with him. You've known him since you started school. You played on the same baseball team in high school. But you're not a friends kinda person."

"You know what I mean. I have my friends from back home, but I don't really have any new friends. Med school is too busy. Work is for work."

"What about at your church? I'm friends with all the ladies at mine."

"I guess I'm friends with people there," Tyler said as he rubbed his chin. "I never really thought about them that way."

Sissy sighed. "Well tell me about the party. How did it go?"

"Fine," Tyler said, stepping into his one-word default setting.

"Did you see Dakota?" she asked. She hadn't heard from him in a few days, and she made a mental note to call him later.

"Yes."

Why did Tyler always sound so rigid and matter of fact when she was trying to carry on a conversation? It felt more like carrying the conversation along with a heavy backpack.

"Was he okay?" she questioned, wishing he'd tell her anything about how her brother had actually been holding up.

"I don't know."

"I talked to Lindsey the other night. She was having a rough time. You know, I wonder about those two all the time. Why are they fighting this?" Sissy said with her hands in the air. "I mean, we all know they're meant to be together. I wish those two would just communicate. They're obviously still in love and hurting each other for no good reason."

Tyler nodded, but it seemed more like he was moving on autopilot instead of agreeing with her.

"I just hate living separate lives around the people I love." Sissy kept her gaze on Tyler, waiting for any reaction to her purposeful use of the L word. It always got his attention.

Tyler didn't say anything. He was looking everywhere except at her. Whatever was on his mind was too big to be swayed by love talk.

"Are you okay?" she asked.

"I'm fine." He met her gaze, but something was off. He had the look of someone who'd been caught with his hand in the cookie jar.

"Okay. If you say so. What are your plans for the evening?"

"I'm supposed to go fishing with Dakota."

"Oh, good. He'll like that. At least he's staying busy. I worry about him home alone in that house. I love what he did with the place, but it's probably killing him that he doesn't have Lindsey to share it with."

Sissy did the majority of the talking throughout lunch, and while that wasn't new, something felt different. There was a tension, like an invisible wall had been erected between them.

When they stepped outside into the humid midday heat, Sissy squinted and shielded her eyes with a hand on her brow. "Don't forget your sunscreen today. Dakota will probably need some too. If I know the two of you, you'll be out on the lake until dark thirty."

Tyler didn't even crack a smile at her silly southernism. When they reached her car, he said, "I'll call you later when I get home."

He leaned in, and she turned her cheek up for him to kiss. "Have fun. I have a full day of laundry ahead of me." She made a sour face that was sure to get her at least a small smile from him.

Instead, he let his hand slip from where it rested on her waist. "Bye," he mumbled as he walked away.

She watched as he made his way to his truck three parking spots away without looking back. Something was definitely wrong, and as much as she wanted to storm over, knock on his truck window, and demand he spill the beans, she couldn't. Her feet were stuck to the ground. Didn't he know he could share anything with her? No problem at work, disagreement with a friend, or difficult health assessment could be made worse by sharing the burden with her, right?

She knew Tyler didn't share her complete and total openness, but there were times like this one when she wished he'd give her more than the few words he'd shared. She would take any glimmer of information that would let her know what was going on inside that intelligent brain of his.

She slipped into the car and closed her eyes. "Lord, I pray that Your protective hand would follow me home. Same for Tyler, please. Keep him safe on the roads. That's a long drive to Carson and back in one day."

With a deep breath, she paused and thought about what was really weighing on her heart. "Lord, whatever has Tyler so worked up, could You please help him fix it? Or help me help him? I don't really know what he needs, but it seems like he needs *something*."

One thing Tyler didn't know about her was that she was a worrier too. She just jumped into help mode instead of getting all pensive like him. Even if it seemed like she didn't have a care in the world sometimes, she most certainly did. It was her natural reaction to face the problem with a smile and an overdose of optimism.

How else did people get through the tough times? She really didn't know.

She blasted the *Mama Mia!* soundtrack on her way home. Her mood was sitting at a steady nine out of ten when she walked through her front door.

A sniffle came from the kitchen, and she peeked her head around the corner to find Christy focused and intent over a mug on the counter.

"Hey, friend."

She took one step before Christy's chin lifted. Her eyes were rimmed in pink with shadowed bags beneath.

"Oh, no," Sissy said as she opened her arms to her roommate. "What happened?"

Christy burst into sobs as Sissy wrapped her in a hug. With her face tucked into Sissy's shoulder, she could barely hear the garbled response.

"What?" Sissy asked.

Christy lifted her head. "Dalton is seeing someone else."

"Nooo," Sissy drawled. "I thought you two were like exclusive or something." They'd been dating for weeks and saw each other almost every night. When did he have time to date someone else when he spent so much time with Christy?

"I thought so too," Christy said, punctuating the fact with a sniffle. "He didn't get the memo."

"I'm so sorry."

"He said he met her around the same time as he met me, and he couldn't decide who he liked more. Really? Like, I thought he really liked *me*. I can't imagine what he was doing with her and then going out with me and acting like it was no big deal." Christy waved her hand dramatically in the air.

"I can't imagine either. If you weren't his first choice, then he wasn't the right man for you."

"I just feel so betrayed," Christy said as she used the end of her oversized T-shirt sleeve to wipe her eyes. "I mean, it's not like he lied to me, but keeping a secret like that feels just as bad."

"Because it *is* just as bad. Secrets are never good in a relationship. Well, unless it's a secret surprise gift or something, but this is *not* a good secret."

"Tell me about it. It's like a knife in my back. I really trusted him, and I feel so stupid."

Sissy wrapped her friend in a tight hug and released

her. "It's good to give people the benefit of the doubt. You can't know until you know."

Christy laughed. "Wow. Astounding advice. You can't know until you know. Profound."

They both laughed again, and Sissy was glad to see that her friend's smile stayed longer this time. "Listen to me, friend. You deserve someone who will cherish you." Sissy placed her hands on both sides of Christy's face, fully capturing her attention. "I repeat. Do not settle for a scrub."

Christy burst into laughter.

"Seriously, there's no way he had time to date you and someone else unless he was unemployed. Scrub, I tell you."

"He did take me on some cheap dates," Christy admitted. "I was stupid enough to overlook it. He said he worked five days a week."

"Say it with me. I don't want no scrub."

Christy laughed and repeated, "I don't want no scrub."

Assured that her point had been made and received, Sissy released the gentle hold on her friend's face. "Now, get some workout clothes on. We're going running. Nothing cute because we're not on the prowl. This is about cheering you up, not catching another man."

"Thanks, friend. I'll be right back." Christy wiped her eyes again and left with a small but genuine grin on her face.

Sissy pulled out her phone on the way to her room to change out of her dress. She sent Tyler a quick text.

Sissy: Have I told you lately how much I appreciate you?

In truth, she was relieved that honesty wasn't an issue between them. The more she thought about how much Tyler respected her, the stronger the urge became to share how she really felt. She loved him without question, and she couldn't wait to tell him.

CHAPTER 16
Tyler

Tyler snuck a glance at Sissy's sketchpad as she drew the meticulous shading of hanging curtains. They'd been watching a documentary about castles of Western Europe, and she'd been flipping back and forth between three different designs, adding touches to each as something on the show sparked her imagination.

"I'm not sure why valances aren't a thing anymore. They're very decorative." She pointed toward the TV with the eraser end of her pencil. "Even the queens of England liked them on their four-poster beds."

Tyler wasn't sure if he agreed or not. Without being entirely certain what a valance was, he couldn't make an educated opinion. "It looks nice there." He pointed to her current sketch.

Sissy patted his cheek and looked adoringly up at him. With her cuddled up under his arm like this, he could lay his head back and easily fall into a deep sleep. Everything felt right when she was beside him.

He'd never taken the time to sit on the couch in the evenings and watch TV. It seemed like a waste of time when he could be reading research results or studying. But with Sissy beside him, it didn't seem like a waste of time. Instead, he'd come to value the easy time with her. He imagined she'd done a good job of teaching him to stop and smell the roses, and for once, he was happy to say he'd been wrong and her way was better.

A knock came from the front door, and they both turned at the sound.

"You expecting someone?" Sissy asked.

"No. I'll be right back." Tyler slid his arm from where it had been tucked behind her and straightened his shirt as he walked to the door.

He opened the door and froze when he saw Dakota. His disheveled hair and lazy stare made him almost unrecognizable as the fun-loving friend he used to know.

"Hey," Tyler said tentatively. "What's up?" Trying to remain calm while Sissy's drunk brother stood at his front step wasn't working at all. The open door blocked her view of Dakota, but Tyler had mere seconds before she found out.

"I tried calling you," Dakota said in a rough voice. He sounded like he had a sore throat.

Tyler's phone was in the kitchen where he'd left it after he and Sissy had eaten dinner. He wasn't on call, and he didn't want any distractions in the few hours he had to spend with her tonight.

Dakota bowed his head and pressed the heels of his hands into his eye sockets. "I don't know what I'm doing. I was going fishing, but I didn't want to go alone. All I do is think when I'm alone. So I called, and you didn't answer, and I just..."

Tyler's breath halted in his throat. "You just drove here from Carson?"

Dakota didn't answer, but he lifted his head, causing him to sway on his feet. "Yeah."

Before the full impact of Dakota's words registered to Tyler, Sissy stepped up behind him. He turned to her instinctually, and she froze. She'd no doubt read the look on his face because her own expression was a mixture of worry and confusion.

"What's wrong?" she asked before peeking around the door to see the haggard image of her brother framed by the dark night.

"Dakota. What are you doing here?" She reached for him, pulling him through the doorway and into the foyer.

"What are *you* doing here?" he growled.

Sissy looked up at her brother as if she didn't recognize the man in front of her. Tyler could smell the alcohol. Everything was about to crash and burn. He just didn't know how bad the fallout would be once it was over.

The haze in Dakota's eyes seemed clearer when he

turned to Tyler. "What is she doing here? Did you tell her?"

Tyler shook his head and opened his mouth to speak, but Dakota interrupted.

"Why is she here? Are you *dating* her? This whole time?" Dakota turned back to Sissy with a hard look on his face.

Sissy frowned back at her brother. "We *are* dating. What's it to you?" She whipped her attention to Tyler, and the unfamiliar, angry expression remained on her face. "Tell me what?"

Tyler stood immobile between Sissy and Dakota. They were both looking at him, waiting for his answers to their barrage of questions, but only one word came to mind.

Guilty.

He'd kept secrets from both of them, and this was the reckoning.

"What didn't you tell me?" Sissy repeated. She locked her attention on her brother. "Are you drunk?" she shouted. "You smell awful, and you look terrible. What's going on?"

She sounded almost frantic now, and any control Tyler might have had left was disappearing. Seeing Sissy worried and confused was tearing his chest apart, and it was all his fault. Well, part of it was Dakota's, but Tyler felt the majority of the weight on his own shoulders.

Dakota's attention bounced back and forth

between Tyler and Sissy as if unsure where to look for answers. "You didn't tell her?"

"No, he didn't, but one of you better start talking." She crossed her arms over her chest and waited, serious and demanding as a school teacher.

Tyler swallowed and stepped closer to Sissy. He laid a gentle hand on her arm, but she didn't move from her firm stance.

"I've been trying to help Dakota. He's been drinking, and he knew he needed help." Tyler glanced at his friend who was staring back with his jaw tight.

"So you got drunk and drove here from Carson? How stupid can you be?" she yelled at her brother. "Drinking? How could you? You could ruin your life or someone else's. You know better!"

"He knew he needed help, so he came to me," Tyler said in the best calming voice he could muster.

"And *you* didn't tell me?" she asked Tyler. The confusion and hurt in her voice made her words crack.

"I promised him I wouldn't tell you, but I should have," he admitted, speaking as quickly as possible.

She was already pulling back, taking small steps away from him. She might as well have been running because he felt her absence like the loss of something vital—an organ or a limb.

"I just... I didn't know what to do. I was trying to help."

"By dating my sister? Yeah," Dakota interjected.

Sissy pointed her finger in her brother's face. "I'm

an adult," she reminded him. "You don't get a say in who I date."

"You didn't even *tell me*," Dakota spat.

"You didn't tell me you were drinking either!" she exclaimed. "Dakota, that's not something to play around with."

"This is why I didn't want to tell you," he said as he linked his fingers behind his neck. "I knew you would just yell at me."

"Because I care! That's not a bad thing. I can't lose you." Her chest rose and fell in heavy waves, and she bit her lips between her teeth. She was on the verge of tears.

"Sissy, listen," Tyler said.

Her attention darted to him, and the moisture in her eyes slid down her face in rushing drops. Her expression was fury and hurt, and the sight of her pain sent a jolt through his chest like a hammer plunging its way through a concrete wall.

"How could you keep this from me? About my brother? You know I wanted to help him. I didn't know it was this bad!"

Tyler took a step toward her, but she took an equal step back. He reached for her, but she held up a halting hand.

Tyler scrambled for the words to make this right. He needed at least one word that might help. "I'm sorry. I should have told you. I should have been there more for him." He pointed at Dakota.

She nodded, and when she spoke, her words were

steady and sure. "You're right. You should have told me."

He took another step toward her, but she shook her head and stepped back again.

"I appreciate you trying to help him, but I don't appreciate secrets. He's my brother. I had a right to know. I was with you almost every day. I talked to you about how much I worry about him, and you could have told me at any time that he needed more help. I could have spent the summer in Carson and helped him." She shook her head and whispered, "I feel like you two lied to me."

He couldn't deny it. It *was* a lie. A lie of omission was still a lie, and of course the unfalteringly honest woman in front of him would see it that way.

Sissy's chin dropped a fraction, and she wiped the tears from her cheek. "We could have worked together to help him. We both care. But the two of you pushed me out." She inhaled deep, looking almost defeated.

Tyler wanted to run to her and wrap her in his arms. It killed him to see her so heartbroken and upset over something he'd done.

She sucked in a ragged breath. "I just care about him, and I want to help him. I lost my dad. I can't lose Dakota too."

Tyler looked around as if there might be a way to fix this mess he'd made. Instead, he found himself searching for someone who was missing. "Where is Dakota?"

Sissy's eyes widened. "Did he leave?"

No, he couldn't have left. Tyler had been so focused on repairing what he'd destroyed with Sissy that he hadn't heard Dakota slip out.

Sissy grabbed Tyler's sleeve. "He left! He's on the road!" Her voice was high-pitched and frantic.

Tyler placed his hands on both sides of her face, willing her to focus on him. "We'll find him. Get your stuff, and let's go."

They darted in opposite directions. Tyler grabbed his phone from the kitchen and keys from the hook beside the front door. Sissy found her purse in the living room and jogged out the door seconds before Tyler.

"I'll drive," Tyler said.

"Not a chance. I'm not riding with you," Sissy spat.

The words were hot like fire, and for the first time, he realized she wasn't only upset with him, she was furious.

She would never trust him again. She wouldn't be able to forgive him.

He watched her slip into the driver's seat of her car, and he couldn't just stand there while she left him for good.

"Wait!" He rushed over and opened the passenger door of her purple car.

"Whatever. Get in."

He settled into the seat and secured his seatbelt. He couldn't remember the last time he hadn't been the driver of the vehicle he was in, and the lack of control was making his skin crawl.

As if he had any control of the disaster of the last quarter of an hour.

"Sissy, can I just—"

She held up a silencing hand. "No. You can't. You've done enough, and I don't want to talk while I drive."

A hole opened in his chest. He'd lost her, and everything felt fleeting and finite. Sissy was the only thing he'd selfishly wanted to hold onto for the rest of his life. She was a firework against a dark sky, beautiful and magnificent.

But she wouldn't be his, and the realization was crippling.

Sissy pulled out onto the road and began on the path that led to their hometown.

CHAPTER 17
Sissy

Sissy angrily wiped at the tears on her cheeks. She hated all of these feelings—helplessness, worry, and hurt. They'd left her out. She wasn't sure why, but the betrayal hurt the worst. Was it because they didn't think she was serious or responsible enough to handle a situation of this magnitude?

When would everyone stop treating her like a kid? She *did* care about important things. She *could* be trusted to show up and do what was expected of her. She *wasn't* irresponsible. Did she really deserve to be lied to just because she was a fun and happy person?

Apparently, her ability to look on the bright side wasn't winning her any awards with this crowd.

And Dakota. How had she misjudged his situation so drastically? She would do anything for him. Didn't he know that?

And Tyler. She wasn't thrilled to have him sitting beside her right now. For once, she didn't want to hear a single word from him. They hadn't finished their conversation, but that was okay with her. She didn't need closure just yet, and she wasn't ready to make nice. She wanted time to be mad about it first.

This must be what real anger felt like, and it was frightening. It was changing her. She could feel the dark hole in her chest, and she didn't know what to do with it.

Confusion filled her thoughts in the darkness as she drove. She'd been so happy with Tyler only an hour ago, and now she didn't know what to think.

Then sadness crippled her. Losing Tyler would be the hardest lesson she'd ever learn. He might be an arm's reach away, but this wasn't the Tyler she'd fallen in love with.

She needed to focus on finding Dakota.

One thing at a time. Breathe in. Breathe out.

She dredged up the basic problem-solving steps she taught the kids she babysat. First things first, call for help.

The first person who came to her mind was her brother's friend, Jake Sims. He was a deputy in their hometown, and he'd know how to get the search party coordinated.

"Can you call Jake?" she asked without taking her attention off the road.

He pulled out his phone and put it on speakerphone. Jake answered on the second ring. "Jake Sims."

His direct greeting reaffirmed her decision to call

him. He'd get right to business helping her find Dakota.

"Jake, it's Sissy. Dakota is somewhere between Atlanta and Carson, and he's been drinking. Please help me find him." Her words cracked, and she felt the shaking in her jaw that let her know tears were on their way.

"I'm on it. I'll keep you posted."

"Thanks." There was a second, silent thanks in there for not asking why she was calling from Tyler's phone. One thing at a time, she reminded herself again.

The call ended, and before Tyler could put his phone down, she asked. "Can you call my mom?"

Tyler did as she asked without hesitation.

There wasn't any sign of Dakota's Bronco on the road. Maybe he was just heading home and he would make it on his own.

Ugh. She didn't want to think about the alternative. How could he be so stupid?

And the realization hit her straight in the chest. Maybe that's why he hadn't told her. The only thing she wanted to do was reprimand him, and perhaps that wasn't what he needed. Apparently, Dakota needed more help than she realized, and maybe she couldn't fix this.

There were three short rings before her mother's welcome voice filled the dark cab. "Hello."

"Mom, Dakota's in trouble." Without warning, the waterworks began anew.

"What's happened?" Her mother's tone was more alert.

"Please let me drive," Tyler whispered.

Sissy shook her head. "I don't know. He's on the road, and he's been drinking, and I don't know what to do."

"Where are you?"

Sissy sniffed. "I'm looking for him now, and Jake is looking too. He's somewhere between Atlanta and Carson."

The silence on the line was enough to send Sissy into a panic. "Mom?"

"I'm here." Her reply was low and barely controlled.

Sissy took a deep breath and tried to clear her mind. "Can you go to his place and wait for him? Let me know when he makes it there if I don't catch up to him first?"

"Yes. That's a great idea. Please keep me posted. I'll be praying."

"Me too. Pray hard."

Her mother didn't need to be told that, but Sissy needed the reminder. She'd jumped in the car so angry and upset that she'd forgotten the most important thing.

"I love you," her mother said, adamant and bold.

"I love you too."

Her mother disconnected the call, and Sissy took another deep breath. She could only do so much, and she hoped it was enough.

Her phone dinged, but she couldn't check it while she was driving. "Can you get that?"

Tyler picked up the phone. "It's Declan."

"Declan? He's stationed in Texas." She couldn't imagine why he'd be texting her.

"It says 'Where are you?'"

"Tell him where we are," she said.

Sissy heard the ding of Declan's response, but Tyler was silently staring at the phone.

"What does it say?"

"He said he's on the phone with Dakota. He's had a wreck, and he might be somewhere near Lincoln."

Sissy's blood felt cold in her veins. It was her worst fear, losing someone else she loved. The fear stole the breath from her lungs.

"Why did he call Declan and not us?" she asked. Declan was the one person who *couldn't* help Dakota right now. Surely, he knew that she and Tyler weren't far.

Tyler's words were hollow. "I don't know."

"We're not far from Lincoln," Sissy said. "At least we know where he is. Can you call Jake and tell him?"

Tyler made the call asking Jake to send paramedics and any other help they might need. Sissy stayed silent this time. Worry and confusion swirled within her until she wanted to vomit. They needed to find him soon. Her breaths came in shorter bursts as she scanned the road illuminated by her headlights.

"I'm sorry," Tyler muttered.

"What if we don't find him in time?" Sissy cried,

ignoring his apology. Tears flowed down her cheeks again.

"We'll find him." Tyler's tone was absolute, but she didn't trust it.

She didn't trust anything right now.

"If he's wrecked, we should have caught up to him by now. It's been too long," she said as she sniffed. "Will you pray?"

Tyler began speaking instantly. She could hear him, but only one of the words registered in her mind.

Help.

Wasn't that the prayer she'd asked for summed up in one word?

Tyler was still praying when her headlights landed on Dakota's Bronco.

"There!" she shouted and parked as far off the road as she could without sliding into the ditch herself.

The front of the truck was smashed into a thick oak tree.

She hit the flashers as she scrambled to get out of the car.

"Wait," Tyler shouted as she closed the door behind her.

She didn't wait. Tyler could wait. Everything else could wait. Dakota needed her now.

Dakota needed more than she could give him right now.

She looked both ways down the dark road before sprinting toward Dakota's truck. The tall grass beside the road tickled her ankles, and her chest burned. She suppressed the urge to scream as her body crashed into the driver's side door.

"Kota!"

Blood was on the side of his face, and his eyes were open but tired.

"Don't move him!" Tyler shouted behind her.

"Sissy," Dakota whispered.

"I'm here," she stammered. Her throat was tight, and the tears were back. "I'm here. Help is on the way."

No sooner than she'd said the words, the whine of an ambulance siren pierced the night. She looked up to see the colored lights flashing across the trees.

She turned back to Dakota as Tyler reached her side. In a matter of minutes, she'd be forced to leave his side to let the professionals help him. "I should've been there for you. I should've helped you. I wish I could take your pain away." She sniffed and brushed a hand over the side of his face unmarked by blood. "You mean the world to me."

Tyler's hands rested on her shoulders, and she slowly turned to him as two EMTs approached the vehicle with bags. More emergency vehicles arrived, and Sissy allowed Tyler to lead her away from the scene.

She stopped by her car and leaned her back against it. With her head bowed, she prayed softly, blocking everything else out with her fervent requests for help and guidance.

When she lifted her head, they were pulling

Dakota from the vehicle. The team worked like a well-oiled machine, anticipating each other's movements as they transferred him to a gurney.

Tyler stood silently beside her, watching her like a hawk.

If he was waiting for her to say something profound that would fix this, he could just keep waiting. She opened the car door. Digging around in the console, she found her cell phone.

"I'm going to see where they're taking him." She walked off without waiting for a response.

When the EMT verified the hospital, she called her mom to let her know where to meet them. They were taking him back to Atlanta, and their mom would have at least an hour's drive.

When she disconnected the call, she turned to find Tyler waiting beside her.

"Can you take my car? I'm going to ride with them." She hooked a thumb over her shoulder toward the ambulance.

"Sure." He accepted the keys from her but didn't press for more.

"Thanks. I just need to grab my purse." She walked away from him, needing space and silence to purge her heavy emotions.

CHAPTER 18
Sissy

Sissy sank onto Dakota's couch and tucked a blanket around her legs. She settled the laptop on her thighs and opened to her favorite home goods shopping site. During the last week she'd been staying with Dakota, she'd poured her energy into finishing up the interior decor. Half a dozen packages had arrived today, and she'd given each piece a new home.

Dakota didn't care about the rugs or the wall hangings, but she needed something to keep her busy. Focusing on things she could control kept her mind off the things she couldn't.

She was lonely. Dakota had been sleeping a lot since he came home from the hospital, and she'd already cleaned out the pantry and restocked the fridge.

She didn't find any alcohol. Her experience with alcoholic behaviors was minimal, but she'd expected to find some secret stash. It seemed booze didn't last long enough around here to warrant a home.

Before long, she'd fallen into a dazed scrolling state. Apparently, emotions were draining. She'd never been so tired before this week. Worrying was exhausting.

Her cell phone dinged beside her.

Lindsey: You feeling better today?

Sissy picked up the phone and rotated it in her hand while she contemplated her reply. Her friend thought she was sick. Laryngitis was the only lie she could come up with that would excuse her from talking to her best friend all week.

Lie. She was lying just like Tyler and Dakota had done. But she'd lied so she didn't have to tell Lindsey about Dakota's wreck. That was sparing her feelings and possibly her career. If Lindsey knew Dakota was laid up in bed with broken ribs and a ruptured spleen, she'd be on the first flight back to Georgia.

She'd spend her savings, miss work, and probably lose her apartment.

No, Lindsey didn't need to come back like this. If she came back to Dakota, it needed to be her choice.

Sissy: Still not the best. Thanks for checking on me. You ok?

Lindsey: I'm good. Just missing your face.

Sissy: Love you.

Lindsey: Love you. Hugs.

Sissy tossed the phone onto the couch beside her and stretched her neck. She was beginning to get stir crazy in this house. Maybe she needed to make another run to the grocery store.

After putting her laptop aside, she tiptoed down the hallway to Dakota's bedroom. Easing the door open, she saw he was asleep and closed it. She'd be back before he woke. He'd need pain medication soon, and she'd hidden everything from him. She didn't care one bit if it was overkill. She wasn't taking any chances. How would she know if alcoholics were also predisposed to other addictions?

With her purse strap secured over her shoulder, she stepped out onto the porch. The air was growing cooler by the day as fall approached, but the trees hadn't lost their verdant radiance. Taking a deep breath, she made a note to open the windows more. Fresh air would be good for Dakota.

The drive into town was short, and the parking lot at the grocery store was packed. In her faded T-shirt and yoga pants, she was guaranteed to see no less than a handful of people she knew in the next half hour.

When she pulled her phone from her pocket to check her grocery list, she saw that she had a missed call from Marie.

She pressed the number to call her back and forgot the grocery list. It wasn't like she really needed anything here. It was all about escaping her wandering thoughts.

Marie's sweet voice answered, "Hello."

"Hey. Sorry I missed your call."

"No problem. I was just calling to check on your brother."

Sissy pushed the cart into the produce section. "He's the same. Grumpy that he's bedridden and can't take care of himself."

"How are you holding up? Can I bring you anything?"

"I appreciate it, but I'm fine. I'm at the grocery store now because I need to stretch my legs."

"Have you been out to do anything for yourself?" Marie asked.

"No, but I can't think of anything I'd want to do." The circumstances had her sitting around in a funk most of the time, and she wasn't a fan.

Marie sighed. "Have you talked to him?"

"No. And I... I don't know if I want to." In truth, Sissy wasn't sure about anything right now.

"Honey, I love you. That's why I'm going to be honest with you."

"Here we go," Sissy whispered.

"You're not perfect."

Sissy stopped pushing the cart. "That's mean."

"No, it's the truth. You like the truth, right?"

"Well, yeah." She did when Marie wasn't knocking her down a peg.

"Sometimes, the truth isn't pretty. Sometimes, you just need to keep the truth to yourself."

"Hold on a second. I know you're not saying it was okay for Tyler and Dakota to keep this from me."

"I'm not saying that. But I am saying they were trying to spare your feelings."

Sissy strolled out of the produce section and up an aisle of paper products. Was walking without knowing where you were going a common thing? Because she'd never done it before today.

"I know he isn't a bad guy," Sissy admitted. "But I'm not happy with him."

"Another truth: I'm not always happy with David, but I don't throw the baby out with the bath water."

"I don't even know what that means," Sissy admitted.

"It means a relationship isn't worth quitting because you had a fight."

"It was a pretty big one, in case I need to remind you."

"I'm not trying to tell you what to do, but I think you should pray about it."

Sissy had been praying, but had she prayed about how to handle the situation with Tyler? She'd been so wrapped up in pushing all thoughts of him from her mind that she hadn't considered forgiving him.

And that truth had her chest aching. She wasn't perfect, and neither was Tyler. But the Lord called her to forgive others as He forgives her.

Sissy still hadn't responded when Marie continued, "Don't listen to me. Listen to Him."

"I think I really messed up," Sissy whispered.

"We all do. I just know that you would both feel

much better if you could forgive him. I'm not saying you have to continue your relationship."

Sissy exhaled in a rush and turned her cart to the checkout lanes. "Thanks. For everything. I'm not handling this well."

"Honey, I think you're doing your best. This is a tough time for you on multiple accounts. Keep your chin up."

"I miss you. I miss the kids." Her mood always improved when she was around the Wilson kids. Maybe a few hours surrounded by their joy would revive her lost happiness.

"You can come back whenever you're ready. We all miss you too."

"I'll call you tomorrow."

Sissy spotted a table with white boxes on top, and she barely heard Marie's farewell. Pushing the cart toward the display, she tried not to hope it was what she thought it was—what she needed.

Sure enough, the boxes had Joe's Donuts written on the top. She grabbed a box and moved to the closest open checkout line.

"Hey, Trudy. What kind are these?"

Trudy's white hair was pulled back into a bunch, and her reading glasses hung from a string around her neck. "Original glazed." She tilted her head and furrowed her brow. "You okay?"

Sissy felt her chin quiver. "Yeah. I was just hoping for sprinkles."

"I hope glazed will at least do you a bit o' good."

Trudy leaned over to peer into Sissy's cart. "You not getting anything else?"

"No, just this." Sissy placed the box on the conveyor belt and pulled out her wallet.

Trudy scanned the barcode and tapped on her register. "Three dollars."

Sissy handed over the bills and picked up her box of medicine. Donuts were the treatment for a broken heart.

Trudy held out the receipt. "Hang in there, sweetie. He's gonna be fine."

Sissy nodded. Everyone in town knew about Dakota's wreck and the circumstances behind it. They also knew about his sentencing for the DUI—community service and a hefty fine.

There weren't any secrets in Carson, and she was beginning to believe that wasn't always a good thing.

"Thanks. Keep the prayers coming."

Trudy laid a hand on her chest. "I love that boy. If you need anything, call me."

"I will. Have a good one."

In the quiet of her car, Sissy tore the plastic wrap off the box and opened it. She inhaled the sweet smell of baked sugar and grabbed the sticky donut.

By the time she'd finished the snack, she felt much better. Sugar might actually be good medicine. Feeling bolder and clear-headed after her conversation with Marie, Sissy picked up her phone and opened the messaging app to Tyler's contact. Where to start?

She typed the message and hesitated.

One word.

But she knew which word he'd choose. *Sorry.*

He'd already apologized. She'd heard it and promptly dismissed it.

Two wrongs didn't make a right, and now she owed him an apology too.

She sent the message and stared at her phone, waiting for a reply.

When she'd eaten another donut without a reply, her heart felt heavy again. Maybe there was too much damage to be repaired between them.

CHAPTER 19
Tyler

Tyler reached above his head to pull the painters tape from the crease between the wall and ceiling in his dad's shed. He and his dad had spent the day painting the interior, and now they had a day's worth of work ahead of them putting everything back on the walls.

His dad had a nice workspace. If Tyler had chosen a different career path, he might have enjoyed woodworking beside his old man.

"Elvis is in the building!"

Tyler didn't have to turn around to know Brian had decided to join the task force. "How's it goin'?"

"Smooth and steady." Brian linked his hands behind his head and studied the cluttered room. "You got a job for me?"

Tyler stepped down from the ladder and tossed the wad of blue tape into the trash can. "Dad'll be back in a minute. He can tell us where he wants all this stuff."

Brian nodded and looked everywhere but at Tyler. "So, you and Sissy."

"Yep." Tyler was getting used to being confronted about his unexpected relationship with Sissy. Every mention of her name hit harder than the last.

"Wanna tell me the story?" Brian coaxed.

Tyler sat on a nearby stool and reached into the cooler for water. He tossed one to Brian and kept the other for himself. "Not much to tell."

Brian huffed and leaned against the workbench Tyler and his dad had moved to the center of the room. "You're no fun."

"I've been told."

"Exactly. And Sissy is fun. Just wondering how that ever worked."

Tyler took a drink of the water, trying to swallow the lump in his throat. "I wonder that myself."

"When did it happen?"

"A few months ago. The beginning of summer, I guess."

Brian crossed his arms over his chest and stared at Tyler, patiently waiting for him to crack like an egg and spill his insides.

Tyler rubbed his brow and thought about how he and Sissy had gotten together in the first place. "I don't know. She kind of elbowed her way into my life. I didn't have much of a choice."

Brian gave a single, deep laugh and rubbed his chin. "That sounds about like Sissy. She's a few years younger than me, and you're what, four years older than I am?"

"Yep. There's that too."

"But I mean, I don't think it's a crazy idea. She could be good for you."

Tyler lowered his head and picked at the label on the bottle of water. "I've heard that before too."

Brian slapped a heavy hand on Tyler's back. "Maybe it's not over. It sounds like y'all had a good thing goin'."

"Before I screwed it up."

"Sissy isn't one to hold a grudge. Y'all could make up."

"You're talking about it like I pulled her ponytail. I kept a pretty big secret from her."

"We all did," Brian reminded him. "For the same reason. She's a helper. Sometimes at her own expense."

Tyler shook his head. "There's nothing wrong with that."

"No, but I think you were saving her from herself."

"That's the thing. She doesn't need saving. She would've handled things with Dakota better than I did. I didn't give her enough credit."

"Did you tell her that?" Brian asked.

"No. I didn't."

"Maybe you should."

Tyler looked at his friend. Brian's jokester demeanor was gone, replaced by a beacon of wisdom. "When did you grow up?"

"I didn't. Sometimes, I like to pretend I know what I'm talking about."

Tyler's phone dinged, and he pulled it from his pocket. His heart felt as if it stopped in his chest when he read the message.

Sissy: One word?

"Is that an opportunity calling?" Brian asked.

Tyler didn't want to text her. He wanted to see her smile and wrap his arms around her.

He stood and playfully punched his friend in the shoulder. "Yep. I've gotta go."

"Go get 'em, tiger!" Brian cheered.

Tyler met his dad in the driveway. "I have to run to Dakota's house for a little bit."

"Take your time. I see Brian made it."

"Thanks, Dad."

"Tell Sissy and Dakota I said hello," his dad shouted.

Everyone in town knew Sissy had been staying with her brother since the wreck. All of Dakota's friends had been by to visit and deliver meals except Tyler. He felt like his place in Dakota and Sissy's inner circle had disappeared.

Not today. He had a word for Sissy Calhoun.

* * *

After speeding to Dakota's house, Tyler got out of the truck and almost lost his nerve. What if she shut the door in his face?

But what if she didn't?

He took a deep breath and sprinted up the porch steps. Pausing at the captivating blue door, he knocked instead of just walking in like he normally would. Closing his eyes, he slowed his breathing and tried to clear his head. If he thought about it too much, he wouldn't be able to speak in full sentences, and Sissy liked it when he was open. He could do that for her today.

Open and honest.

The door flung open, and he was staring at Sissy. He was elated and terrified. No amount of breathing exercises could have made his mouth open and say words.

"Hey." The word was too soft. Too quiet to be coming from Sissy.

"Hey." Tyler rubbed the back of his head. "I... Um..."

Sissy moved aside. "Come in."

That was a start. At least his feet were in the door. He wrung his hands and looked around. The living room was fuller than the last time he'd been here. Lamps and rugs covered places that had once been bare.

It was Sissy. She'd been adding her touches.

"He's in the bedroom," she said, pointing toward the hallway.

Once again, he was torn between his friend and his girlfriend. Which one to face first?

His decision was made for him when Sissy stepped

past him into the kitchen. Even after she started the sink and began washing a skillet, he still couldn't bring himself to move.

Closing his eyes, he prayed for guidance and took the first step toward Dakota's room.

The door was open, and Tyler stopped to rap his knuckles against the doorframe.

Dakota perked up when he heard the knock and saw his friend standing in the doorway. "Hey, man."

"Hey."

"Come on in," Dakota said as he tried to sit up straighter.

Tyler tucked his chin and studied his hands. "I'm sorry."

"For what?" Dakota asked. "I'm pretty sure I owe you a huge apology."

Tyler huffed and rubbed the back of his head. "I couldn't help you when you needed me."

"Dude, you're so backwards. My mess-ups are not your fault."

"No, they're not, but I should have been a more attentive friend."

Dakota shook his head. "You went above and beyond the call of duty. I appreciate you. Even more so since I've been talking to Sissy."

Tyler froze, unsure how to react. He had no idea what she'd said about him.

"I'm lucky to have so many friends who care about me." He rolled his eyes. "And I'm glad I have a mouthy sister who cares way more than she should."

Tyler nodded. "I can't argue with that."

Dakota sighed. "What I'm trying to say is that I think... I wish I'd gotten to see the two of you together. She won't talk about you much, but I see that you were doing all you could for me. I just wasn't listening."

"I think it was more bossing than talking. I kinda get why you brushed off my attempts to help."

Dakota chuckled. "I knew you were direct and to the point when I asked for your help. I thought that was what I needed." He rolled his eyes and let his head fall back. "If you tell her I said this, I'll deny it till my dying day. But I think I needed Sissy's kick in the pants more than anything."

Tyler's eyes widened. "I can get behind that."

"You know, she has this way of always knowing what to do and how to help." Dakota waved his hands in the air. "She's scary good at listening. And understanding."

"Are you saying my degree is worthless?" Tyler jested.

"You gotta be kidding. You're too smart for your own good."

Tyler tsked. "Not smart enough to keep the girl."

Dakota huffed. "Same."

They'd both messed up and lost someone. Now Tyler knew firsthand what it was Dakota had been going through. Loving Sissy and then losing her was the hardest thing he'd ever gone through in his life.

"At least you still have a shot," Dakota said. "I

think it helps that I was the dumb one. If she can forgive me, I think she can forgive you too. We both left her out."

Tyler shrugged. "I can only hope."

Dakota tilted his chin up and yelled, "Sissy! Get in here!" He winced after the exertion.

Tyler's thumping heart mirrored her stomping steps down the hallway. She burst into the room with a scowl that would've made Tyler cower if it were aimed at him.

"I am not at your beck and call!"

Dakota shrugged. "But you're here, so please have a good heart-to-heart with my friend."

Sissy's frown softened. Her shoulders relaxed as she turned to Tyler.

"All this is my fault. Tyler told me to tell you, and I wouldn't listen. I asked him not to tell you. He wanted to." Dakota hung his head. "I was worried about disappointing you, and then I went and did something worse. I put myself and others in danger, I took up all your time this past week, and I broke your trust in Tyler and myself. I never meant to do any of that, but it happened anyway. All of it is my fault."

The room went silent, and Tyler cut his gaze to Sissy.

She crossed her arms and lifted her chin. "You were pretty stupid."

Dakota nodded. "Fair enough."

Sissy blinked a few times before looking at Tyler.

Her beautiful smile still hadn't returned. "Can we talk?"

He could only nod. Talking was a great start, if he could only get his mouth to work.

Sissy walked out into the hallway, and Tyler followed her.

When they reached the living room, she burst into tears. Seeing Sissy cry was a harrowing experience. His arms went around her, and she rested her forehead against his chest. They didn't speak. Her sobs were the only sound he heard while his heart broke.

He took three deep breaths before convincing himself to take the plunge. Holding her arms, he stepped back, putting some distance between them so she could see his face.

"I'm sorry. I wish there was some better word I could use to tell you how sorry I am. My life has been turned upside down since you came into it, and that's a good thing."

Her gaze lowered, and he brushed a thumb over her wet cheek. Tears didn't belong there.

"I know I'm hard to love. I don't say or do things like I should, and I'm wrong too often to be as stubborn as I am."

Sissy chuckled, and the beginnings of a smile tugged on her lips.

"But if there's one person I want—no, need in my life, it's you," Tyler vowed. "You want one word? Love. It's love. I love you, and I don't ever want to lie to you or keep secrets. I trust you with everything, and I know you would have been a better counselor to Dakota than I was. He's lucky to have a sister like you, and I was stupid enough to keep a secret that mattered so much to you."

Sissy stared up at him with wide eyes. He couldn't read the expression on her face, and fear gripped him like a vise.

"Love," she whispered. "Love is the one word you choose?"

Tyler searched her features, and he still couldn't figure out what was going through her head. This must be what she'd dealt with in the beginning of their relationship. Not knowing what she was thinking was driving him insane.

The only thing he knew to do was nod.

Sissy smiled up at him. "I love you too. I'm sorry, and I was wrong," she said adamantly.

Tyler stared at her, unable to comprehend what she'd confessed. "I love you," he said again. "And I don't know how you were wrong."

"I know you were doing the best you could. I'm glad you tried to help Dakota. I was keeping a secret too. I didn't tell my brother about us when I knew he'd want to know. It didn't seem like a big deal at the time, but now I see it in a different light."

Tyler shook his head. "Stop it. None of that matters. Dakota knows now. We all kept secrets, and we all learned our lesson."

Sissy huffed. "I sure did."

"You better believe I did too. I'm never keeping a

secret from you again. I'll tell you what I had for lunch every day if you want."

She laughed, and it made his heart light. She loved him, and that was something he'd never experienced before. He was good at pushing people away as fast as they came, but this—what he had with Sissy—was different.

He slid his hands into her hair and leaned down to press his mouth to hers. The weight lifted from his shoulders as they moved together. When her arms wrapped around him, he tightened his grip in her hair.

This was the love of a lifetime, and he would protect it at all costs for the rest of his days.

Epilogue
SISSY

Sissy whistled the tune of "Whistle While You Work" as she stuffed clothes into her overnight bag. It had been months since Dakota's wreck, and his outlook on life had improved with his healing injuries. Though she hadn't worried for a while now that he'd fallen off the wagon, she still liked to lay eyes on him every once in a while. Thankfully, she was making this weekend trip home to Carson solely because she wanted to, and not because she needed to check on him.

The worry may never disappear completely, but she slept easier at night confident that Dakota would let her know if he needed help, and they could handle anything together.

A knock sounded at the front door, and she checked the time on her watch. Who was visiting before eight in the morning?

"Coming!" she yelled as she wrapped her long hair into a messy bun on her way to the door.

She checked the peephole first. She'd watched enough true crime documentaries with Christy to know not to open the door before finding out who was on the other side.

She gasped when she saw Tyler through the distorted lens and jerked the door open. He was grinning before she tackled him with a hug.

"What are you doing here?" she asked as she squeezed her arms tighter around his neck.

"I took the day off."

Sissy jerked back, sure she'd misheard. "You what?"

"The whole day," he confirmed. That gorgeous smile she'd come to love beamed bright.

"Is everything all right?" she asked.

Tyler never took the day off. In fact, he found every excuse to work more. After seeing his passion for healing and helping others, she encouraged him at every turn.

"Yes. I think." Tyler scratched the back of his head. "I wanted to catch you before you headed to Carson."

"You're in luck. I was about to walk out the door."

Tyler nodded and averted his gaze. "Well, would you mind if I kept you just a bit longer?"

Sissy tilted her head and smiled. He knew she'd do anything for him. Why the nervousness? "I wouldn't. What's on your mind?"

Tyler inhaled a deep breath and knelt on the

cracked concrete that made up the tiny porch of her old rental house.

Sissy gasped and covered her mouth. "Tyler Hart, are you proposing?" she screamed.

Tyler winced. "I don't think they heard you in Phoenix. Did you just steal my proposal?"

She danced on her toes, and her hair bobbed in the bun atop her head. "No! I'm just excited!"

Excited was an understatement. She was over the moon.

Tyler chuckled. "Are you ready now?"

"Yes, yes. Go ahead." She waved her hands at him to proceed.

"Melanie Calhoun, you turned my world upside down."

"Good start." She nodded vehemently and her smile stretched.

"Let me do this!" Tyler pleaded.

"Okay, okay. You do it." She made a motion as if locking her lips and throwing away the key.

"Who am I kidding? I'm not good with words. Will you marry me? Be my wife? Grow old with me? Start a family? Will you do life with me?" He took her hands and held them gently. "I love you."

"Are you done?" she asked.

"Yes, I'm finished. It's your turn."

"Yes!" She threw her arms in the air and jumped up and down, no doubt waking the neighbors.

"Wait." Tyler tried to restrain her long enough to capture her hand again. "I have a ring."

"That's great." Without waiting for the ring, she got down on both knees. Grabbing his face in both hands, she kissed him hard, wishing the happiness inside her could somehow flow into him so he could understand her elation.

When she broke the kiss, Tyler held up the ring.

"It's beautiful," she said as moisture filled her eyes.

"You didn't even look at it."

"I don't care what it looks like. It's beautiful, I love you, and we're getting married."

Tyler took her hand and slid the ring onto her finger. "About that. I took off work today."

"You took off work to propose? Is there a second act or something?"

His thumb rubbed circles over her hand, and his attention stayed on her hands. "I was actually thinking, maybe, if you wanted, that we could get married."

"Well, yeah. I just said yes."

"I mean... Well, this is stupid."

Sissy narrowed her eyes. "Marrying me is stupid? Um, I'll have you know I'm quite a catch."

"No, not that. I mean, yes, that. But what I was thinking is we could get married today."

Sissy's eyes widened and she gasped. "Today? Really?"

"If it's stupid, you can just forget I said it."

"Oh no. You're not getting out of this one." She gasped when an idea came to her. "We could elope!"

"That's kind of what I was thinking," Tyler confirmed.

"What made you think of that?"

"It sounded like something you'd do. You know, impulsive and all."

"You would really do that?" Sissy asked in a high-pitched tone.

Tyler's intense gaze held hers, unwavering and strong. "With you? I'd do anything with you."

The heat in his gaze could have set the house on fire, and she would gladly go down in flames with him. He'd effectively stolen her voice.

He leaned closer, and his gaze held hers. "I want to marry you. Today. Then I want to love you tonight and every other night of my life."

Was it possible for a heart to explode with happiness? It seemed possible when her chest was too tight to contain the happiness within it.

She could do that—love him for the rest of her life. Loving him now was almost more than she knew how to comprehend.

It would take a lifetime to show him how much he meant to her.

Other Books By Mandi Blake

Blackwater Ranch Series

Complete Contemporary Western Romance Series

Remembering the Cowboy

Charmed by the Cowboy

Mistaking the Cowboy

Protected by the Cowboy

Keeping the Cowboy

Redeeming the Cowboy

Blackwater Ranch Series Box Set 1-3

Blackwater Ranch Series Box Set 4-6

Blackwater Ranch Complete Series Box Set

Wolf Creek Ranch Series

Complete Contemporary Western Romance Series

Truth is a Whisper

Almost Everything

The Only Exception

Better Together

The Other Side

Forever After All

Love in Blackwater Series

Small Town Series

Love in the Storm

Love for a Lifetime

Unfailing Love Series

Complete Small-Town Christian Romance Series

A Thousand Words

Just as I Am

Never Say Goodbye

Living Hope

Beautiful Storm

All the Stars

What if I Loved You

Unfailing Love Series Box Set 1-3

Unfailing Love Series Box Set 4-6

Unfailing Love Complete Series Box Set

Heroes of Freedom Ridge Series

Multi-Author Christmas Series

Rescued by the Hero

Guarded by the Hero

Hope for the Hero

Christmas in Redemption Ridge Series

Multi-Author Christmas Series
Dreaming About Forever

Blushing Brides Series
Multi-Author Series
The Billionaire's Destined Bride

About the Author

Mandi Blake was born and raised in Alabama where she lives with her husband and daughter, but her southern heart loves to travel. Reading has been her favorite hobby for as long as she can remember, but writing is her passion. She loves a good happily ever after in her sweet Christian romance books and loves to see her characters' relationships grow closer to God and each other.

Acknowledgments

Thank you for reading *A Thousand Words*. I hope you enjoyed Sissy and Tyler's story. This is my fifteenth book, but this story was always planned. It's the prequel to the Unfailing Love series which is complete with six books, including stories for Tyler's friends, Declan, Dakota, Jake, Marcus, Brian, and Tyler's brother, Ian.

I would love to thank my friends who made this book possible. My beta readers, editor, cover designer, and advanced reader team all worked for months to bring everything together. I couldn't do this without their help.

I'm so glad you took a chance on this book. I would appreciate it if you could review this book on Amazon or any other place you like to tell other readers about books.

Just As I Am
UNFAILING LOVE SERIES BOOK ONE

She's running from trouble, but a fake relationship with a kind stranger might give her the protection she needs and a love she never expected.

Declan King has lived a life of solitude and duty for the U.S. Army. When the deaths of his grandparents bring him home to his family farm, he is forced into contact with people who know too much about his past to simply leave him alone.

Adeline Rhodes makes a daring escape from her controlling boyfriend, planning to hide out in the small town of Carson, Georgia. When Addie's past catches up to her, she finds herself thrust into a fake relationship to protect her from her vengeful ex.

As Addie and Declan's chance meeting begins a journey that heals old wounds, they struggle to stay ahead of the danger and deny their growing attraction to each other.

Declan will do anything to protect her, and failure isn't an option when Adeline's life is on the line.

Made in the USA
Columbia, SC
05 October 2024